W9-BLU-926

CAVEBOY
DAVE
NOT SO
FABOO
by Aaron Reynolds
illustrated by Phil McAndrew
VIKING

VIKING
An imprint of Penguin Random House LLC
375 Hudson Street
New York, New York 10014

First published in the United States of America by Viking,
an imprint of Penguin Random House LLC, 2018

LIBRARY OF CONGRESS CATALOGING-IN-PUBLICATION DATA IS AVAILABLE
ISBN 9780147516596 (paperback)
ISBN 9780451475480 (hardcover)

Manufactured in China

1 3 5 7 9 10 8 6 4 2

To Gail Fleming, a super faboo leader
who practically invented creativity! —A. R.

For my Granny, Susan McAndrew, who loves to read
more than anyone else I've ever known. —P. M.

CAVEBOY
DAVE

1

Hi, I'm Dave.
Dave Unga-Bunga.
And this . . . is Bleccchh.

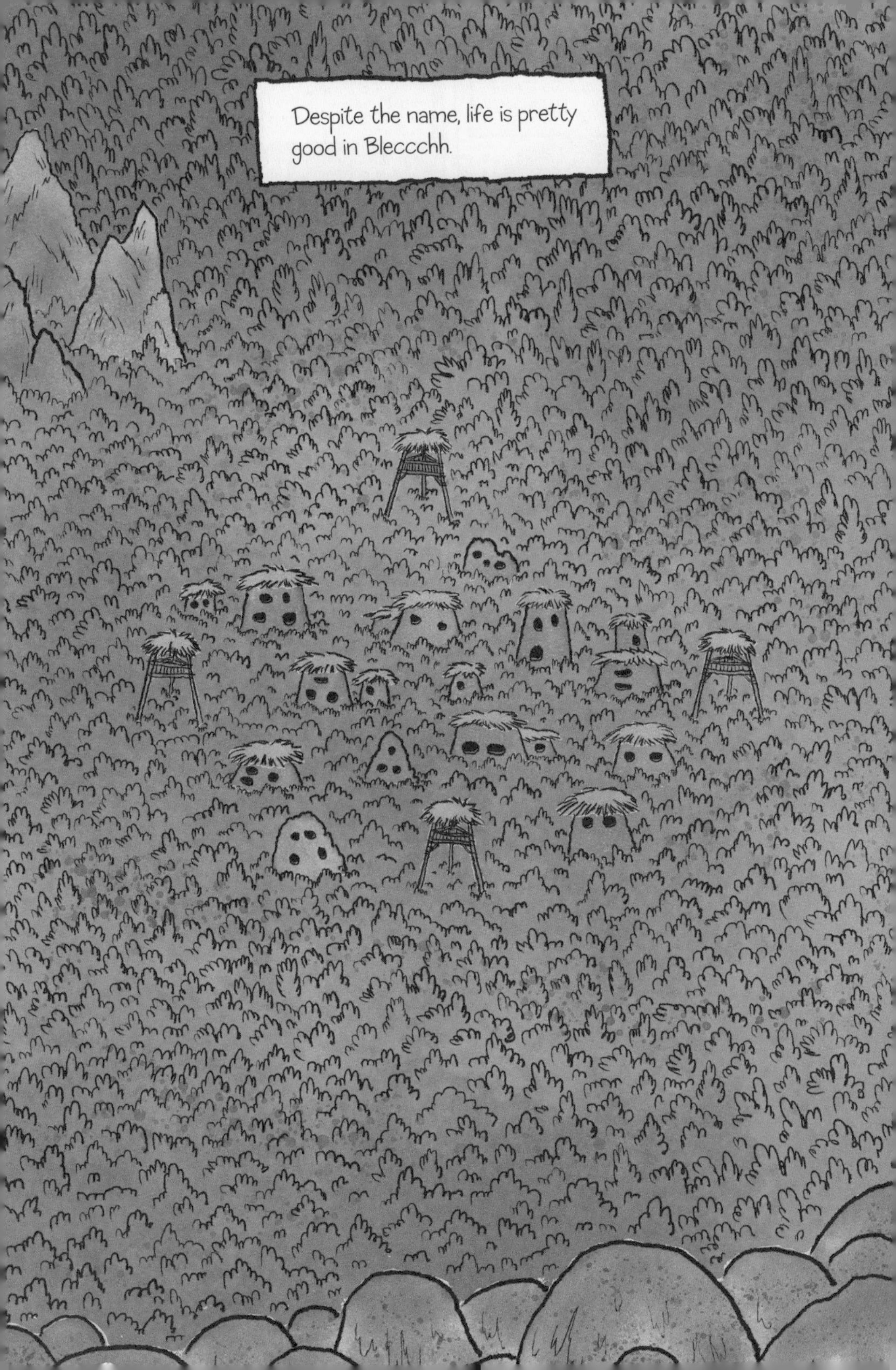
Despite the name, life is pretty good in Bleccchh.

We have watch towers. To keep us safe. (My invention.)
We have summer vacation. To keep us rested. (My invention.)
And my newest invention . . . the ice cream truck.
ICE CREAM!
Just look how happy everybody is!
I don't like to brag, but I may be the best inventor EVER.

BIG D, YOU ARE THE **WORST** INVENTOR EVER!
Then again, maybe not.
WHEN ARE YOU GOING TO INVENT ANOTHER FLAVOR BESIDES **"DIRT"?**
Leave it to Rockie to keep me on my toes.
LIKE WHAT?
HMM. WHAT ABOUT ICE CREAM WITH DIRT AND MARSHMALLOWS?
WHAT ARE MARSHMALLOWS?
NO IDEA, D. YOU'RE THE INVENTOR! **INVENT THEM!**
YEAH, LET ME JUST ADD THAT TO MY TO-DO LIST.

DAVE! GET UP HERE!
BRO! YOU'VE GOTTA SEE THIS!
I GUESS INVENTING MARSHMALLOWS WILL HAVE TO WAIT.
WELL, DON'T WAIT TOO LONG. MY TONGUE IS STARTING TO TASTE LIKE THE BOTTOM OF A FOOT.

C'MON, DWEEB!
This is Bane. 75% chest hair. 23% muscle.
And 2% brain.
BRO, YOU'RE GONNA MISS IT.
I'm not being mean. It's just basic math.
And that's Ug. He's . . . well, he's 100% Ug.

Everybody over twelve has to take a shift on the watch towers. Shaman Faboo's orders.
WHO LIKES THEIR BELLY RUBBED?
ME! I TOTALLY LIKE BELLY RUBS!
Putting Ug and Bane in charge of village safety might not be the best idea.
But hey. Nobody died and made me shaman.
Like I said, life in Bleccchh is comfortable.
But step one foot outside Bleccchh, and you risk being torn to pieces by horrible, deadly, bloodthirsty beasties.
WHOA. GET READY TO SOUND THE ALARM IN CASE IT HEADS THIS WAY.
FEAR NOT, COMPADRE. THAT THING IS MILES OFF.

BIRDS FREAK ME OUT. THEY'RE SO DANG . . .
BIRDY?
EXACTLY.
WHOA!
I CAN'T BELIEVE IT CAUGHT AN ENTIRE POKEYHORN!
POKEYHORN SNACK PACKS ALL AROUND!
I'VE ALWAYS SAID . . . "DON'T MESS WITH A RIPPY-BEAK."
NO TRUER WORDS WERE EVER SPOKEN.
EXCEPT "DON'T WIPE YOUR BUTT WITH A CACTUS."
THOSE THINGS WILL MESS YOU UP.

WAIT. IT'S LANDING ON BALANCING BOULDERS? THAT'S NOT GOOD.
RELAX. THOSE ROCKS HAVE BEEN THERE FOR, LIKE, A KAJILLION YEARS.
ONE LITTLE RIPPY-BEAK ISN'T GONNA TOPPLE THE STACK.

SEE? YOU WORRY TOO MUCH.
I WORRY **EXACTLY** THE RIGHT AMOUNT.

IT LOST THE POKEYHORN! ALL THAT WASTED MEAT!
MEAT?! WHO CARES ABOUT MEAT? BALANCING BOULDERS IS GONE!
IT'S PROBABLY BURIED UNDER TONS OF RUBBLE. I BET I COULD DIG IT OUT.
WHAT ARE WE GOING TO CALL IT NOW? ROCK-SLIDE HEAP? THAT'S A TERRIBLE NAME!
ACTUALLY, I'VE NEVER EATEN RUBBLE. MAYBE IT TASTES GOOD.
HOW ABOUT GEORGE? I'VE ALWAYS LIKED THAT NAME.
YOU. STOP NAMING ROCKS. WE'RE NOT CALLING IT GEORGE.
I NEVER GET TO CALL ANYTHING GEORGE.
YOU. STOP DROOLING. YOU'RE NOT EATING THAT POKEYHORN.
I NEVER GET TO EAT RUBBLE-COVERED MEAT.

BESIDES . . . YOU'RE BOTH MISSING THE MOST IMPORTANT THING.
WHAT?
THAT!
Balancing Boulders had been there forever.

Now that Balancing Boulders was gone, I saw something.
AW. LOOK AT THAT CUTE LITTLE CLOUD.
THAT'S NOT A CLOUD. THAT'S A BONFIRE.
And it was making me worry. Just the right amount.
YOU KNOW WHAT A BONFIRE MEANS.
YEAH. ANIMALS HAVE FINALLY LEARNED HOW TO CAMP OUT.
NO. IT MEANS THERE'S ANOTHER VILLAGE OUT THERE.
WHAT OTHER VILLAGE? WE'RE THE ONLY PEOPLE FOR MILES AND MILES.
OR ARE WE?
DUHN,
DUHN,
DUHNNNNNN!
RAWR.
WE SHOULD PROBABLY SHOW THIS TO SHAMAN FABOO.

ONE STEP AHEAD OF YOU, DWEEB!

OW.
THAT WAS ALMOST AWESOME.

NEXT TIME, TRY IT LIKE THIS.
I CALL IT THE STOPPYDROPPY.
I GET IT! 'CAUSE IT STOPPYS YOU FROM DROPPYING!

Another village meant the great big world had just gotten a whole lot smaller.
And possibly more dangerous.
But maybe Ug was right. Maybe I was worrying too much.
So why did my guts feel like they'd just got run over by an ice cream truck?

2

Shaman Faboo's house.
FABOO

SHAMAN FABOO!
WE SAW SMOKE ON THE HORIZON!
FLOP
SHAMAN FABOO!
BALANCING BOULDERS
FELL DOWN!
SHAMAN FABOO!
MAN, YOU HAVE GOOD
TASTE. LOOK AT
THIS PLACE.

SHAMAN FABOO
GONE
FABOO
SHAMAN FABOO! GONE?
SHAMAN FABOO
GONE
SHAMAN FABOO GONE!!!!!
SHAMAN FABOO
GONE

Thankfully, my dad arrived.
He'd take charge of the situation.
SON? WHAT'S GOING ON, BOY?
DAD, THE SHAMAN IS GONE!
SHAMAN?
I ALREADY DID THAT, DAD.
Or maybe he'd just do everything I already did.
It's sometimes hard to tell with grown-ups.

WHAT'S GOING ON, D?
THE SHAMAN IS MISSING.
SHAMAN FABOO IS GONE?
SHAMAN FABOO IS GONE?
HE'S NOT IN THERE.
I KNOW. I TOLD YOU, I ALREADY LOOKED IN THERE.
IS HE COMING BACK?
IS HE GONE FOREVER?
WHAT WILL WE DO?

CALM DOWN, MRS. MUKLUK. EVERYBODY, PLEASE! THERE'S ONLY ONE THING TO DO IN THIS SITUATION.

AAAAAHHHHHHHHHHHH!!
That wasn't it.
AAAAAHHHHHHHHHHHH!!
Everyone just needed to calm down.
But everyone was too busy screaming to calm down.

QUIET!!!
THIS IS NO TIME TO PANIC.
THE SHAMAN IS MISSING! I'M NO EXPERT, LITTLE MAN, BUT THIS SEEMS LIKE THE **PERFECT TIME TO PANIC!**
WE SAW **SMOKE** COMING FROM THE FOREST!
BALANCING BOULDERS WAS **DESTROYED!**
AREN'T YOU TWO SUPPOSED TO BE ON WATCH?
WELL, YEAH. BUT EVERYONE WAS PANICKING. WE FELT LEFT OUT.

BALANCING BOULDERS IS DESTROYED???
THE FOREST IS ON FIRE???
AAAAAHHHHHHHHHHH!!
KNOCK IT OFF!

YES, BALANCING BOULDERS FELL OVER.
NO, THE FOREST ISN'T ON FIRE. THERE'S A BONFIRE OUT PAST BALANCING BOULDERS.
FROM WHO? WE DON'T HUNT THAT FAR NORTH.
THERE MUST BE OTHER PEOPLE OUT THERE.
OTHER PEOPLE?
I CAME HERE TO TELL SHAMAN FABOO.
GONE
AND YOU FOUND THIS NOTE.
"SHAMAN FABOO GONE."

SHAMAN FABOO IS MISSING.
MYSTERIOUS.
VAGUELY THREATENING.
AND, IF YOU ASK ME, THERE'S ONLY ONE THING TO DO WHEN YOUR SHAMAN GOES MISSING AND YOU FIND A MYSTERIOUS AND VAGUELY THREATENING NOTE LEFT BEHIND.
AAAAAHHHHHHHHHHH!!
NOT THAT!

I THINK . . . MAYBE THE BEST HUNTER SHOULD GO LOOK FOR HIM.
GOOD THINKING, LAD. THAT'S HERSHEL.
Hershel Gronk was my gym teacher.
Despite my distaste for gym class, I had to admit it . . . Mr. Gronk was the most experienced hunter.
MR. GRONK.
MAYBE YOU COULD TAKE A COUPLE OTHERS AND GO LOOK FOR THE SHAMAN?
YOU'RE TELLING ME WHAT TO DO?
Mr. Gronk was the one usually telling *me* what to do.
Run ten extra laps. Do fifty extra push-ups. Get off the floor and quit panting.
JUST A SUGGESTION, REALLY.
RIGHT. GOOD SUGGESTION.

CLUNK! YOU'RE WITH ME.
CLUNK HIT STUFF?
MAYBE, CLUNK. MAYBE.
CLUNK LIKE HIT STUFF.

AND, MR. GRONK?
YEAH?
DO IT QUIETLY.
WHY? WHAT'S WRONG?
DUNNO. BUT THAT BONFIRE HAS ME FEELING UNEASY.
RIGHT. WE'LL BE AS SNEAKY AS SLUGS.

Mr. Gronk would find Shaman Faboo.
If not, the village could decide what to do from there.
It was a decent plan. As good as any.
THAT'S SOME LEVEL-HEADED THINKING, BOY. WELL DONE.
YEAH! BUT WHAT IF SHAMAN FABOO IS GONE FOREVER?
YEAH! I'M OLD! I NEED SOMEONE TO TELL ME WHAT TO DO!
YEAH! WHO'S GOING TO LEAD US?

I KNOW! LITTLE DAVEY CAN LEAD US!
WHAT?
YEAH! DAVE WILL TELL US WHAT TO DO!
NO.
YEAH! DAVE IS IN CHARGE!
NO!
BUT YOU JUST DID IT, D!
WELL, I HAD TO DO SOMETHING! YOU WERE ALL RUNNING AROUND SCREAMING!
AND YOU WEREN'T.
YOU KNEW EXACTLY WHAT TO DO, MAN.

I WAS MAKING THAT STUFF UP!
OH, DAVEY, YOU'RE ALWAYS MAKING GOOD STUFF UP.
SALAD BAR. DAVE MADE THAT UP.
SALAD BAR GOOD.
ICE CREAM TRUCK!
I LOVE ICE CREAM TRUCK!
YEAH, BUT THAT'S DIFFERENT.
THE COMMUNITY HAS SPOKEN, LITTLE DAVE.
THE COMMUNITY IS CRAZY, MRS. MUKLUK. I'M ONLY TWELVE!

I'M GOING HOME. YOU GUYS CAN RUN AROUND AND SCREAM NOW IF YOU WANT TO.
BUT DON'T.
YOU GOT IT, BOSS.
STOP THAT! GAH!
The people in my village were good people.
But boy, could they panic. It was a miracle we hadn't gone extinct yet.
DO NOT EAT MUSHROOMS

Of course, there were still eight hours of daylight left. . . .

Plenty of time to go extinct before bedtime.

3

All I wanted was to go to my room
and quietly work in peace.

Good thing I invented the door.

WELL, LOOK WHO'S MR. WHOOP-DE-DOO!
WELL DONE, BOY!
Then again, peace and quiet were probably super overrated.
BLA! DAD! I'VE TOLD YOU TO KNOCK FIRST!
KNOCK
KNOCK
PLEASE GO AWAY!
WELL, LOOK WHO'S MR. WHOOP-DE-DOO!
WELL DONE, BOY!
Nobody listens to me around here.

BLA, LET'S GIVE YOUR BROTHER SOME SPACE.
THANK YOU!
WHAT HAPPENED TO GIVING ME SOME SPACE?
BY THE SPEARHEAD OF CHUK-CHUK! I'M SO PROUD OF YOU, SON!
Note to self: Invent the door lock.
I DIDN'T EVEN DO ANYTHING.

SHAMAN DAVE! YOU'LL BE THE YOUNGEST SHAMAN IN HISTORY!
THAT'S NOT HAPPENING! AND QUIT PLANNING MY WHOLE LIFE WITHOUT ME!
YOU SAW WHAT HAPPENED!
YEAH, BUT . . .
BUT NOTHING! THE VILLAGERS ARE READY TO FOLLOW YOU!
NO OFFENSE, BUT THE VILLAGERS WOULD FOLLOW A PILE OF POKEYHORN POO IF IT WORE A LOINCLOTH AND TOLD THEM WHAT TO DO.
DON'T SELL YOURSELF SHORT, LAD. YOU'RE WAY SMARTER THAN POKEYHORN POO.

I DO NOT WANT
TO BE SHAMAN!
WHY NOT?
I DO NOT WANT TO
BE IN CHARGE!
YOU DON'T
HAVE TO
YELL!
NEITHER
DO YOU!!!

LET'S TAKE THINGS DOWN A COUPLE NOTCHES. WHAT'S BOTHERING YOU, BOY?
IT ALL HAPPENED SO FAST! NO ONE EVEN ASKED WHAT I THOUGHT!
THAT'S IT. LET IT OUT.
SHAMAN FABOO IS **GONE!** EVERYONE IS LOOKING AT ME TO MAKE **DECISIONS!**
BECAUSE YOU WERE THE ONLY ONE MAKING CLEAR DECISIONS.
I CAN'T LEAD THE **WHOLE** VILLAGE!

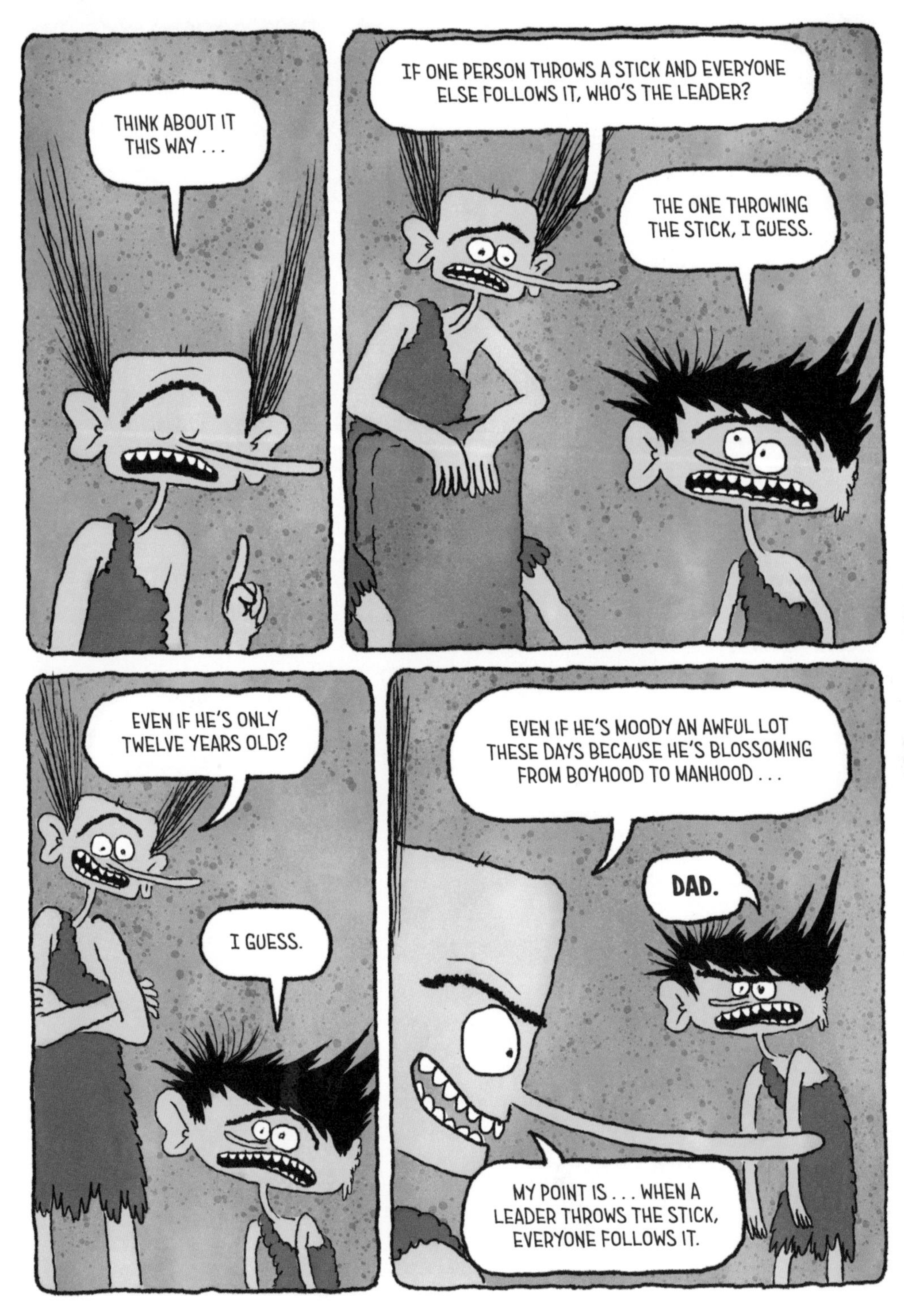

THINK ABOUT IT THIS WAY . . .
IF ONE PERSON THROWS A STICK AND EVERYONE ELSE FOLLOWS IT, WHO'S THE LEADER?
THE ONE THROWING THE STICK, I GUESS.
EVEN IF HE'S ONLY TWELVE YEARS OLD?
I GUESS.
EVEN IF HE'S MOODY AN AWFUL LOT THESE DAYS BECAUSE HE'S BLOSSOMING FROM BOYHOOD TO MANHOOD . . .
DAD.
MY POINT IS . . . WHEN A LEADER THROWS THE STICK, EVERYONE FOLLOWS IT.

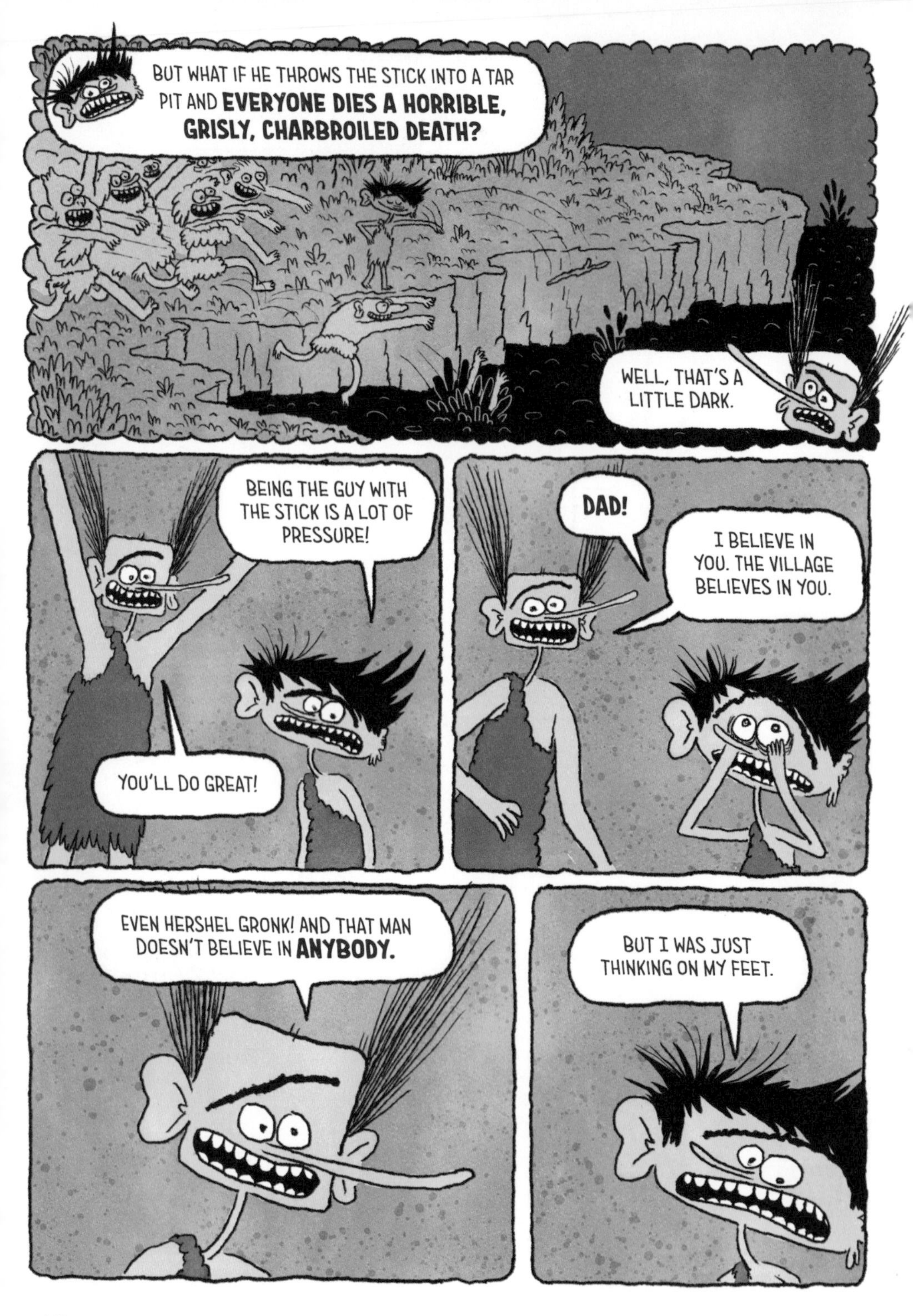
BUT WHAT IF HE THROWS THE STICK INTO A TAR PIT AND **EVERYONE DIES A HORRIBLE, GRISLY, CHARBROILED DEATH?**
WELL, THAT'S A LITTLE DARK.
BEING THE GUY WITH THE STICK IS A LOT OF PRESSURE!
YOU'LL DO GREAT!
DAD!
I BELIEVE IN YOU. THE VILLAGE BELIEVES IN YOU.
EVEN HERSHEL GRONK! AND THAT MAN DOESN'T BELIEVE IN **ANYBODY.**
BUT I WAS JUST THINKING ON MY FEET.

EXACTLY. YOU WERE JUST BEING DAVE.
RIGHT.
AND DAVE IS GREAT AT THINKING ON HIS FEET. THAT'S ALL LEADING IS!
BUT . . .
THAT'S THE SPIRIT, BOY! AS LONG AS YOU ARE YOURSELF, YOU'LL DO **JUST FINE.**
My dad meant well. He just had a bad habit of letting his excitement take over.
Still. Maybe I *was* freaking out for no reason.
Maybe I *could* be the leader that everyone wanted me to be.

SHAMAN DAVE.
I had to admit . . . I kinda liked the sound of that.

4

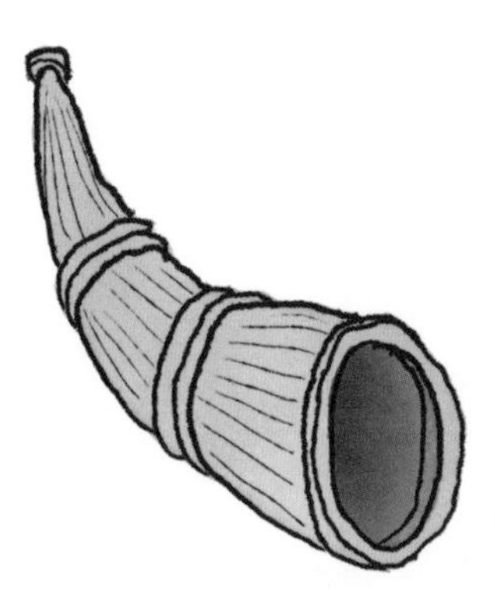

By the next morning, I was feeling a little more confident.

Maybe Dad is right.
Maybe I can do this.
DAD, I THINK YOUR LITTLE PEP TALK PAID OFF.
OF COURSE IT DID!

WHAT LITTLE PEP TALK?
ABOUT BEING IN CHARGE. I SLEPT ON IT, AND I'VE MAYBE CHANGED MY MIND.
SO YOU'RE SAYING I WAS RIGHT.
NO. I JUST DECIDED THAT I AGREE WITH YOU.
SAME THING. LET'S BE HONEST.
I'M GOING TO GIVE IT A TRY.
THAT'S THE STUFF!
I'M GOING TO BECOME THE BOSS OF EVERYBODY!
WELL, I DON'T THINK I PUT IT QUITE LIKE THAT.

BUT I'M GLAD YOU CAME AROUND. JUST DON'T GET TOO BIG FOR YOUR BRITCHES.
WHAT ARE BRITCHES?
NO IDEA. LET'S GO TELL EVERYBODY.
We headed out to round up the village.
But the village found us first.

They had followed me home. Look how much they needed my wisdom.
HI, EVERYBODY!
HEYA, BIG D.
I MADE A DECISION: I WILL BE IN CHARGE, LIKE YOU WANT. AT LEAST UNTIL SHAMAN FABOO GETS BACK.
I'LL BE THE ONE TO TELL EVERYONE WHAT TO DO.
OH, SORRY. I FORGOT TO TELL YOU WHAT TO DO. YOU CAN BURST INTO APPLAUSE NOW.
THAT'S WONDERFUL, DAVEY BOY!

AS A MATTER OF FACT, WE'VE ALSO MADE A DECISION.
OH, YEAH?
WE DECIDED YOU'RE RIGHT. YOU'RE ONLY TWELVE.
HE'S CHANGED HIS MIND ABOUT THAT. TWELVE IS LIKE THE NEW TWENTY-FIVE.
DAD.
YOU'D BE THE YOUNGEST PERSON TO EVER RUN THE VILLAGE.
WHICH IS NEAT, RIGHT? WE'RE MAKING HISTORY HERE!
PLEASE, DAD.
AND WE DECIDED . . . YOU SHOULDN'T LEAD US.

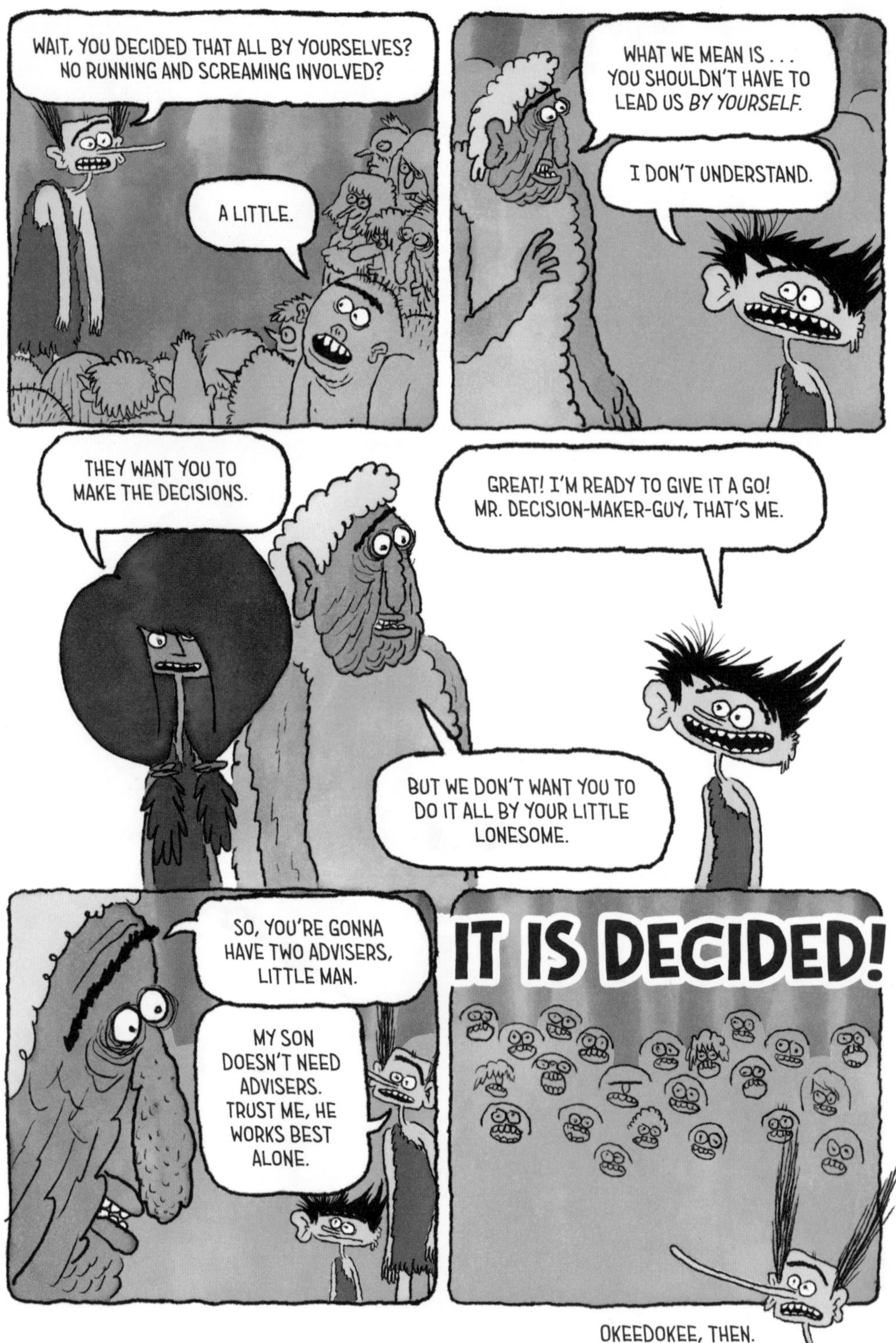
WAIT, YOU DECIDED THAT ALL BY YOURSELVES? NO RUNNING AND SCREAMING INVOLVED?
A LITTLE.
WHAT WE MEAN IS . . . YOU SHOULDN'T HAVE TO LEAD US *BY YOURSELF.*
I DON'T UNDERSTAND.
THEY WANT YOU TO MAKE THE DECISIONS.
GREAT! I'M READY TO GIVE IT A GO! MR. DECISION-MAKER-GUY, THAT'S ME.
BUT WE DON'T WANT YOU TO DO IT ALL BY YOUR LITTLE LONESOME.
SO, YOU'RE GONNA HAVE TWO ADVISERS, LITTLE MAN.
MY SON DOESN'T NEED ADVISERS. TRUST ME, HE WORKS BEST ALONE.
IT IS DECIDED!
OKEEDOKEE, THEN.

YOU'LL PICK ONE ADVISER AND THE VILLAGE WILL PICK THE OTHER.
YEAH, SURE. I GUESS I COULD USE SOME ADVISERS.
YOU PICK FIRST, DAVEY.
PICK ME, DAVE!
RIGHT HERE, DAVE! PICK ME!
DON'T PICK ME, BRO. I HAVE NO IDEA WHAT ANYONE'S TALKING ABOUT.
But I knew who I wanted without even thinking about it.

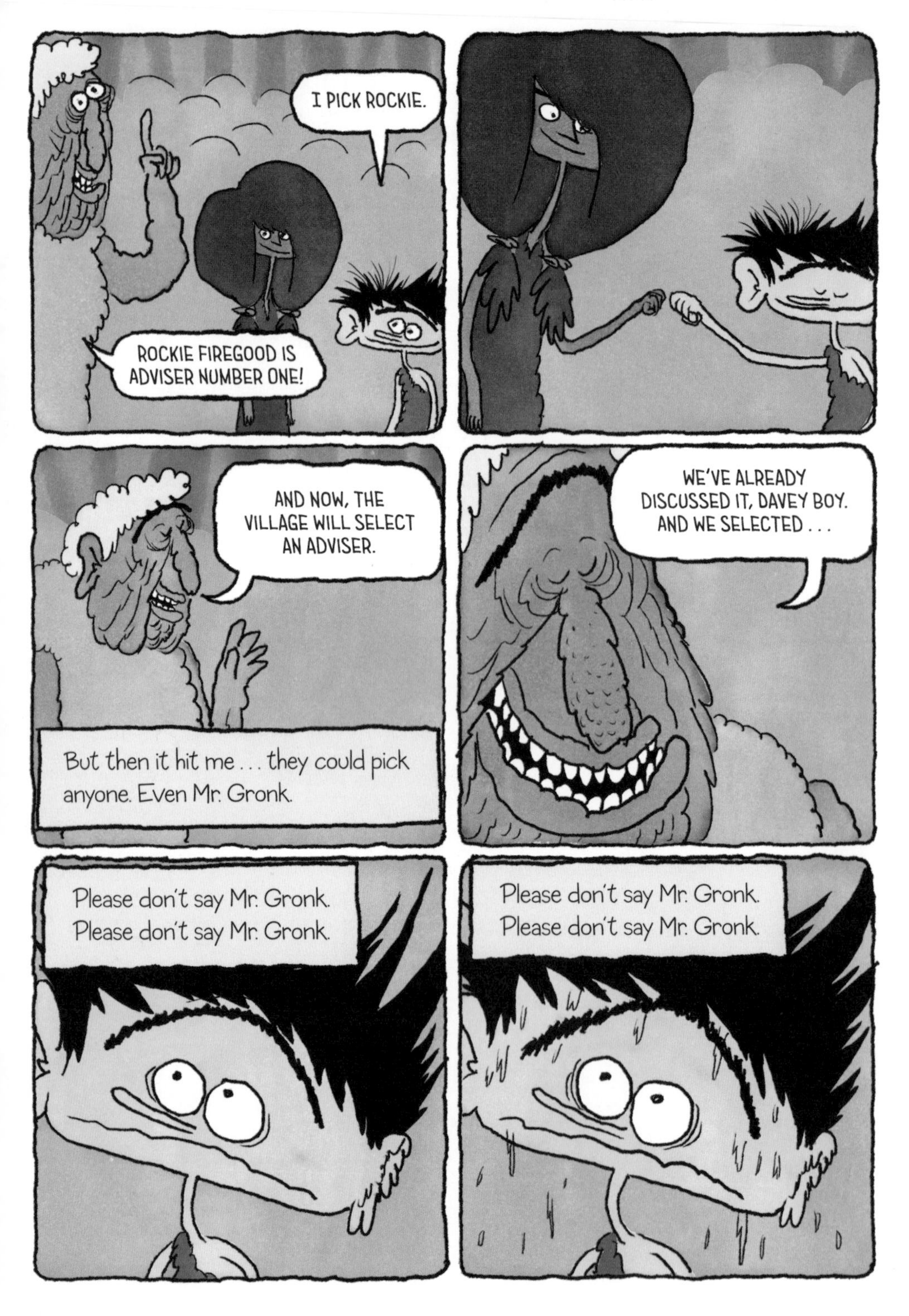
I PICK ROCKIE.
ROCKIE FIREGOOD IS ADVISER NUMBER ONE!
AND NOW, THE VILLAGE WILL SELECT AN ADVISER.
But then it hit me . . . they could pick anyone. Even Mr. Gronk.
WE'VE ALREADY DISCUSSED IT, DAVEY BOY. AND WE SELECTED . . .
Please don't say Mr. Gronk. Please don't say Mr. Gronk.
Please don't say Mr. Gronk. Please don't say Mr. Gronk.

YOUR FATHER.
I'VE ALWAYS SAID . . . THE BOY NEEDS ADVISERS!
WAIT, WHAT?
MR. UNGA-BUNGA IS ADVISER NUMBER TWO!
NO, WAIT. YOU CAN'T PICK MY DAD.
AND WHY NOT, I'D LIKE TO KNOW?
YOUR FATHER IS A WISE AND SAGE MEMBER OF THIS COMMUNITY.
SEE? SAGE!
I KNOW, BUT . . .
HE IS THE INVENTOR OF THE WHEEL. AND THE TORCH!
SEE? TORCH!
I KNOW, BUT . . .

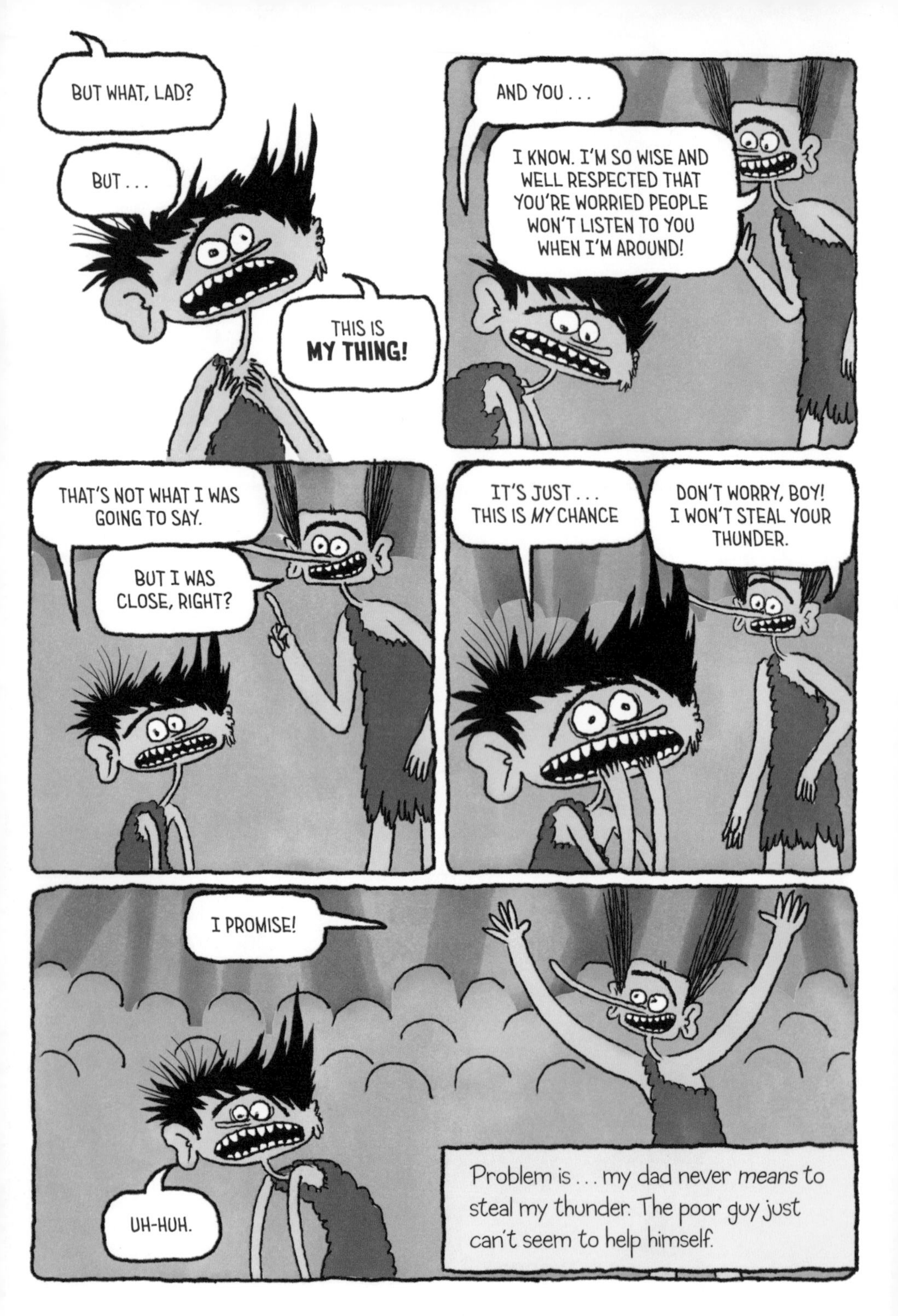
BUT WHAT, LAD?
BUT . . .
THIS IS **MY THING!**
AND YOU . . .
I KNOW. I'M SO WISE AND WELL RESPECTED THAT YOU'RE WORRIED PEOPLE WON'T LISTEN TO YOU WHEN I'M AROUND!
THAT'S NOT WHAT I WAS GOING TO SAY.
BUT I WAS CLOSE, RIGHT?
IT'S JUST . . . THIS IS *MY* CHANCE
DON'T WORRY, BOY! I WON'T STEAL YOUR THUNDER.
I PROMISE!
UH-HUH.
Problem is . . . my dad never *means* to steal my thunder. The poor guy just can't seem to help himself.

IT IS DECIDED!
I GUESS IT IS DECIDED.
UNTIL THE RETURN OF SHAMAN FABOO, WE PRESENT YOU WITH THIS.
A BROKEN SEASHELL?
IT'S THE THREE PIECES OF THE GATHERING HORN.
IT IS?
BEFORE THEY DIED, MY PARENTS CARVED THIS HORN FOR SHAMAN FABOO.
YOU NEVER TOLD ME THAT.
I DON'T REALLY LIKE TO TALK ABOUT IT.
IT'S TRUE. THE FIREGOODS MADE IT FROM THE BROKEN NOSE-HORN OF THE LARGEST POKEYHORN EVER KILLED.

APART, EACH PIECE WILL TRUMPET.
TOOT
BUT WHEN YOU PUT THEM TOGETHER . . .
. . . THEY CREATE THE BLAST THAT BRINGS THE VILLAGE TOGETHER.

WHICH MEANS?
YOU THREE HAVE TO AGREE ON ANY BIG DECISION. SO PLAY NICE.

WE GIVE A PIECE . . .
. . . TO EACH OF YOUR ADVISERS.
AND THE BIGGEST PIECE TO YOU, LITTLE DAVEY.

IT IS DECIDED!
Hmm. I was discovering that this whole "being the boss" thing might not be all it was cracked up to be.
Because it was cracked into three pieces.
And Rockie had one.
And my dad had the other.
ISN'T THIS GREAT, LAD? FATHER AND SON, RULING THE WORLD TOGETHER!

I hate it when my dad has the other.

5

The next day, the smoke on the horizon had disappeared.

And Mr. Gronk still hadn't returned with Shaman Faboo.

WHAT IS TAKING HIM SO LONG?
IT'S ONLY BEEN A DAY!
BE QUIET, BLA.
YOUR SISTER IS RIGHT. PART OF BEING IN CHARGE IS WAITING AROUND.
HEAR THAT? YOUR SISTER IS RIGHT!
BUT WHAT IF SOMETHING BAD HAPPENED TO MR. GRONK? OR CLUNK? OR SHAMAN FABOO? **WE HAVE TO DO SOMETHING!**

YOU WORRY TOO MUCH, LAD. IT'S PRACTICALLY COMING OUT OF YOUR EARS.
WHO WORRIES TOO MUCH?
DAVE DOES! IT'S IN HIS EARS AND EVERYTHING!
I WORRY EXACTLY THE RIGHT AMOUNT, THANK YOU.
WELL, PUT YOUR WORRIES ON PAUSE, BIG D. YOU'VE GOT A CROWD OUT FRONT.
HUH? WHAT DO THEY WANT?
YOU! IT'S THE SHAMAN'S JOB TO SOLVE PROBLEMS THAT VILLAGERS ARE HAVING.
WHAT? THEY'RE **CAVEMEN!** THEY'RE *SUPPOSED* TO HAVE **PROBLEMS!**

Being the boss was turning out to be much more boring than I'd imagined.
HEY, EVERYBODY. UM . . . HEY.
OKAY, EVERYBODY! MAKE A LINE!
YOU! SIT DOWN.
Leave it to Rockie to keep me on my toes.
DAVE WILL HEAR YOU NOW.

HI, MR. STONEWALL. WHAT'S GOING ON?
THIS YOUNG MAN HAS DOODLED ON MY CAVE PAINTINGS! DOODLED!
HE DREW MUSTACHES ON MY HERD OF STOMPYBEASTS! MUSTACHES!
GAK RULES
THAT WAS VERY BAD, GAK.
YEAH, I KNOW.

SO . . . ARE WE DONE WITH THIS ONE?
NO, SON. YOU HAVE TO PUNISH HIM.
WHAT? FOR MUSTACHES?
HE RUINED MR. STONEWALL'S PROPERTY.
YEAH, BUT IN A SLIGHTLY HILARIOUS WAY.
PLUS, HE FEELS TERRIBLE ABOUT IT. DON'T YOU, GAK?
TERRIBLE.
SEE?
IT'S YOUR JOB, BOY.
I DON'T KNOW. YOU'RE KIND OF THINKING LIKE A DAD, DAD.
BUT, DAVE!
LET'S ASK ROCKIE.

WHAT DO YOU THINK, ROCKIE? I VALUE YOUR OPINION.
YOU KIND OF NEED TO PUNISH HIM. IF YOU DON'T, HE'LL PROBABLY JUST DO IT AGAIN.
EXACTLY! SMART GIRL!
GAK, DO YOU PROMISE YOU WON'T DO IT AGAIN?
I PROMISE.
AND YOU REALLY FEEL BAD ABOUT IT?
HORRIBLE.
HE FEELS HORRIBLE, MR. STONEWALL. HOW ABOUT WE LET HIM OFF WITH A WARNING?
I DEMAND JUSTICE! I . . .
PERFECT! CASE DISMISSED!

YOU'RE THE BOSS, BOSS.
ALL RIGHT, THEN.
I JUST HOPE THIS DOESN'T COME BACK TO BITE YOU IN YOUR BOSSY BUTT.
NEXT!
WHAT'S THE PROBLEM, GUYS?
THIS MY LIZARD.
NUH-UH. THIS MY LIZARD.
LET ME GET THIS STRAIGHT. YOU BOTH THINK THIS LIZARD BELONGS TO YOU.
MY LIZARD.
NUH-UH. MY LIZARD.
Oh, boy. Being the boss was turning out to be much more exhausting than I'd imagined.

SON, I THINK . . .
I GOT THIS, DAD.
I had just thought up a clever solution that would make these two see reason.
I SUGGEST WE CHOP THE LIZARD IN HALF.
WAIT, WHAT?
WATCH THIS.

OKAY. CHOP.
UH-HUH. CHOP.
WAIT! WOULDN'T YOU RATHER JUST SHARE THE LIZARD THAN CHOP IT IN HALF?
NOPE. EACH GET HALF.
UH-HUH. EACH GET HALF.
CHOP!

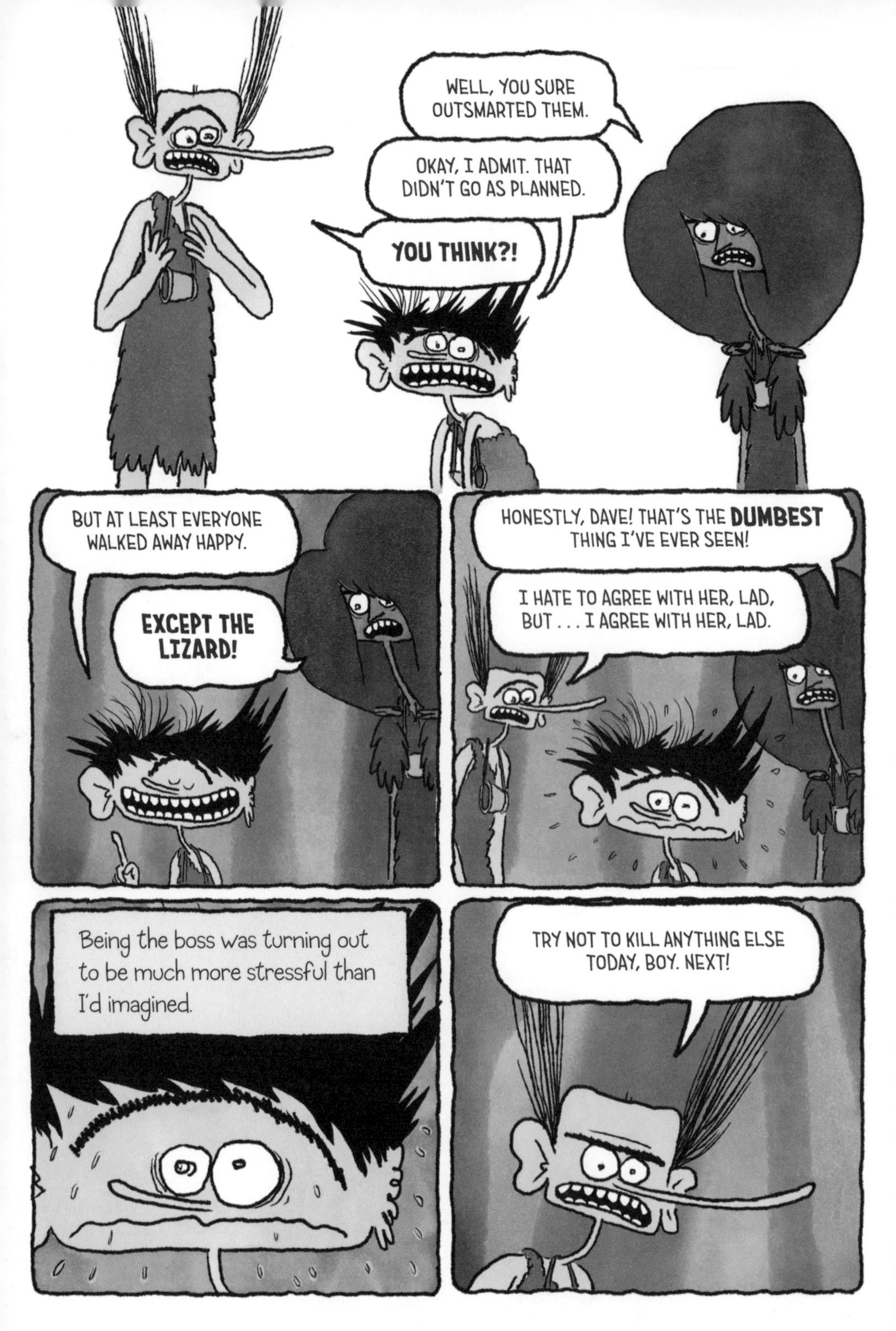
WELL, YOU SURE OUTSMARTED THEM.
OKAY, I ADMIT. THAT DIDN'T GO AS PLANNED.
YOU THINK?!
BUT AT LEAST EVERYONE WALKED AWAY HAPPY.
EXCEPT THE LIZARD!
HONESTLY, DAVE! THAT'S THE DUMBEST THING I'VE EVER SEEN!
I HATE TO AGREE WITH HER, LAD, BUT . . . I AGREE WITH HER, LAD.
Being the boss was turning out to be much more stressful than I'd imagined.
TRY NOT TO KILL ANYTHING ELSE TODAY, BOY. NEXT!

MR. STONEWALL? WE ALREADY SAW YOU, REMEMBER?
I KNOW THAT! I HAVE WRINKLES, NOT AMNESIA!
WHY DID YOU GET BACK IN LINE?
BECAUSE OF HIM! NOW HE'S PAINTED TOP HATS ON ALL MY HUNTERS. TOP HATS!
STONEWALL STINKS

GAK? BUT WE JUST LET YOU OFF WITH A WARNING ONLY TEN MINUTES AGO.
WHAT CAN I SAY, DAVE? I HAVE TO BE FREE TO EXPRESS MYSELF.
I TOLD YOU SO.
YEAH, BUT . . .
I DEMAND JUSTICE!
YEAH, BUT . . .

DAVE! MR. GRONK IS BACK!
RAWR!
THEY'RE BACK?
WITH SHAMAN FABOO?
OH, THANK GOODNESS.
JUST HURRY UP, BRO!
I GOTTA GO, MR. STONEWALL.
WAIT JUST A BONE-PICKIN' MINUTE!
DON'T WORRY. SHAMAN FABOO WILL FIX EVERYTHING FOR YOU.

I wasn't going to admit it to my dad and Rockie, but I was done being in charge.
WHERE HAS HE BEEN?
WHERE DID THEY FIND HIM?
WHAT WAS HE DOING?
UM . . . I BETTER LET MR. GRONK EXPLAIN EVERYTHING.
Who needed the pressure of solving everyone's problems?
I was ready to go back to being a normal twelve-year-old.
Let's face it. That's pressure enough.

6

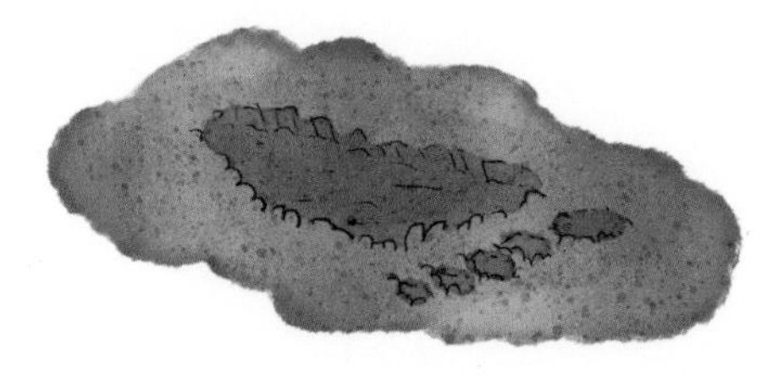

This didn't look good. Mr. Gronk and Clunk looked like they had been dragged behind an ice cream truck for five miles.
I SMELL TROUBLE.
NAH, THAT'S JUST MY FLAME-BROILED ARM.
HERSHEL! WHAT HAPPENED?
WHERE'S SHAMAN FABOO?

DAD. ROCKIE. I GOT THIS.
MR. GRONK! WHAT HAPPENED? WHERE'S SHAMAN FABOO?
WELL, WE STARTED BY SEARCHING AROUND THE SHAMAN'S HOUSE.
WE FOUND SOME FOOTPRINTS LEADING FROM THE SHAMAN'S FRONT DOOR.
AND THEY WERE DRAGGING SOMETHING.
DRAGGING SOMETHING?
OMINOUS, BRO. **OMINOUS.**

THEY LED NORTH THROUGH THE FOREST . . .
AND?
YOU'RE NOT GOING TO LIKE IT.
I ALREADY DON'T LIKE IT.
RIGHT INTO THE FIELD OF SCREAMS.
WHAT?! THAT FIELD IS A DEATH TRAP!
THANKS FOR THE SAFETY TIP, MISSY.

WHAT WERE YOU THINKING, HERSHEL? NOBODY HAS EVER ENTERED THE FIELD OF SCREAMS AND LIVED.
EXCEPT FOR CRISPY JIM.
I SMELL LIKE BARBEQUE!
YEP. CRISPY JIM. AND NOW ME.
WHY DID YOU DO THAT? YOU COULD HAVE DIED!
SO I GOT A LAVA SPLASH TO THE ARM. I'LL PUT SOME ALOE VERA ON IT.

YOU SAID THIS WAS A GOOD IDEA!
WHAT?
YOU SHOULD HAVE TOLD ME NOT TO DO IT!
WAIT . . . NOW YOU **WANT** ME TO TELL YOU WHAT TO DO?
AND LOOK! HE'S HURT!
YOU HEARD HIM. IT'S A VERY MINOR THIRD-DEGREE BURN.
RELAX! I TURNED BACK RIGHT AWAY. NOBODY CAN CROSS THAT MINEFIELD OF DEATH.

SO WAIT . . . WE FIND A MYSTERIOUS NOTE. "SHAMAN FABOO GONE."
YEAH . . . ?
THEN WE FIND TRACKS DRAGGING SOMETHING . . .
RIGHT . . .
. . . OR **SOMEBODY** THROUGH THE FIELD OF SCREAMS. RIGHT TOWARD THE SMOKE.
ARE YOU SAYING SHAMAN FABOO WAS DRAGGED AWAY?
I'M SAYING THERE'S ANOTHER VILLAGE OUT THERE. AND I DON'T THINK THEY'RE FRIENDLY.
THAT'S CRAZY, BRO. YOU WORRY TOO MUCH.
I WORRY EXACTLY THE RIGHT AMOUNT.
HISTORICALLY, THAT IS TRUE.

THEM TAKE SHAMAN?
EXACTLY, CLUNK.
CLUNK GETTING MAD.
ME TOO, CLUNK. ME TOO.
AND NOW I'M GOING TO DO SOMETHING ABOUT IT.
HOLD ON, BOY!
I'M GOING TO RESCUE SHAMAN FABOO.
WHOA, THERE. A GROUP SHOULD GO, LAD. BUT YOU SHOULD STAY HERE.
DAD!
I'M NOT TRYING TO STEAL YOUR THUNDER. OR MESS UP YOUR THINGY.

I JUST DON'T WANT ANYTHING TO HAPPEN TO YOU! I NEED . . . THE VILLAGE NEEDS YOU.
HE'S RIGHT, DAVE.
DAD! ROCKIE! I AGREE! A GROUP SHOULD GO.
WAIT . . . YOU ACTUALLY AGREE WITH US?
YES! BUT IF YOU THINK I'M SITTING HERE LISTENING TO PEOPLE'S PROBLEMS FOR ONE MORE MINUTE, YOU'RE NUTS.
I'D RATHER FACE TWENTY FIELDS OF SCREAMS THAN ONE MR. STONEWALL AGAIN.
YOU SAY THAT NOW. BUT MR. STONEWALL DOESN'T SPEW MOLTEN LAVA.

YOU ARE ONE STUBBORN UNGA-BUNGA. BUT IF YOU INSIST ON GOING, I'M GOING TO BE RIGHT BESIDE YOU.
CLICK
IT'S NOT SMART. SOMEBODY COULD GET REALLY HURT.
Leave it to Rockie to keep me on my toes.
COME ON, ROCKIE. TRUST ME!
I GUESS IT'S THE BEST IDEA WE'VE GOT.
CLICK

LET'S MAYBE KEEP THE WHOLE FIELD OF SCREAMS THING TO OURSELVES.
GOOD IDEA. IT COULD LEAD TO MORE SCREAMING AND RUNNING AROUND.
GOTCHA. LEAVE IT TO ME.

WE HAVE NEW INFORMATION!
YEAH! NOT THE KIND THAT INVOLVES BURNING LAVA!
MR. GRONK HAS RETURNED!
SEE? HE'S RIGHT THERE! NOT EVEN BURNED TO DEATH! AT ALL!
HE HAS DISCOVERED THAT THERE IS A VILLAGE OF OTHER PEOPLE TO THE NORTH.
AND BARELY ANY DEADLY BURNY THINGS STAND BETWEEN US AND THEM!
STOP HELPING, UG.
YOU GOT IT, COMPADRE.
THEY HAVE SHAMAN FABOO!

WHAT? WHY WOULD THEY TAKE OUR SWEET LITTLE SHAMAN?
WE DON'T KNOW WHY THEY TOOK HIM OR WHAT THEY WANT WITH HIM.
BUT I'M GOING TO GET HIM BACK!
Maybe this was a big mistake. Or maybe this was my big chance.
Either way, if I was going down . . . it was going to be in a blaze of gory.
Did I say gory? I meant glory.

MR. GRONK!
YOU WILL STAY BEHIND.
WHAT? YOU NEED ME TO SHOW YOU THE TRAIL!
I NEED YOU HERE MORE. SOMEONE NEEDS TO PROTECT THE VILLAGE WHILE WE'RE AWAY.
CLUNK SHOW TRAIL.
LET ME GET THIS STRAIGHT. YOU WANT ME TO STAY BEHIND WHILE YOU CHARGE OUT TO FACE ALMOST **CERTAIN DEATH???**
YES.
ACTUALLY, THAT SOUNDS PRETTY DARN GOOD.

THE RESCUE PARTY WILL BE ME . . .
CLUNK.
ROCKIE.
MY DAD.
BANE.
AWESOME! I BET I RULE AT RESCUING PEOPLE FROM EVIL VILLAGES!
AND . . .

UG.
BRO. DID YOU MEAN "UGH" OR DID YOU MEAN "UG"? BECAUSE THEY SOUND A LOT ALIKE.
I MEANT YOU.
IF YOU MEANT "UGH, I CAN'T TAKE UG," I TOTALLY UNDERSTAND.
I MEANT YOU.
UGH.
DON'T WORRY, EVERYBODY. THE NEXT TIME YOU SEE US, WE'LL HAVE SHAMAN FABOO!
EITHER THAT, OR WE'LL BE CRISPIER THAN CRISPY JIM.
I SMELL TOAST!

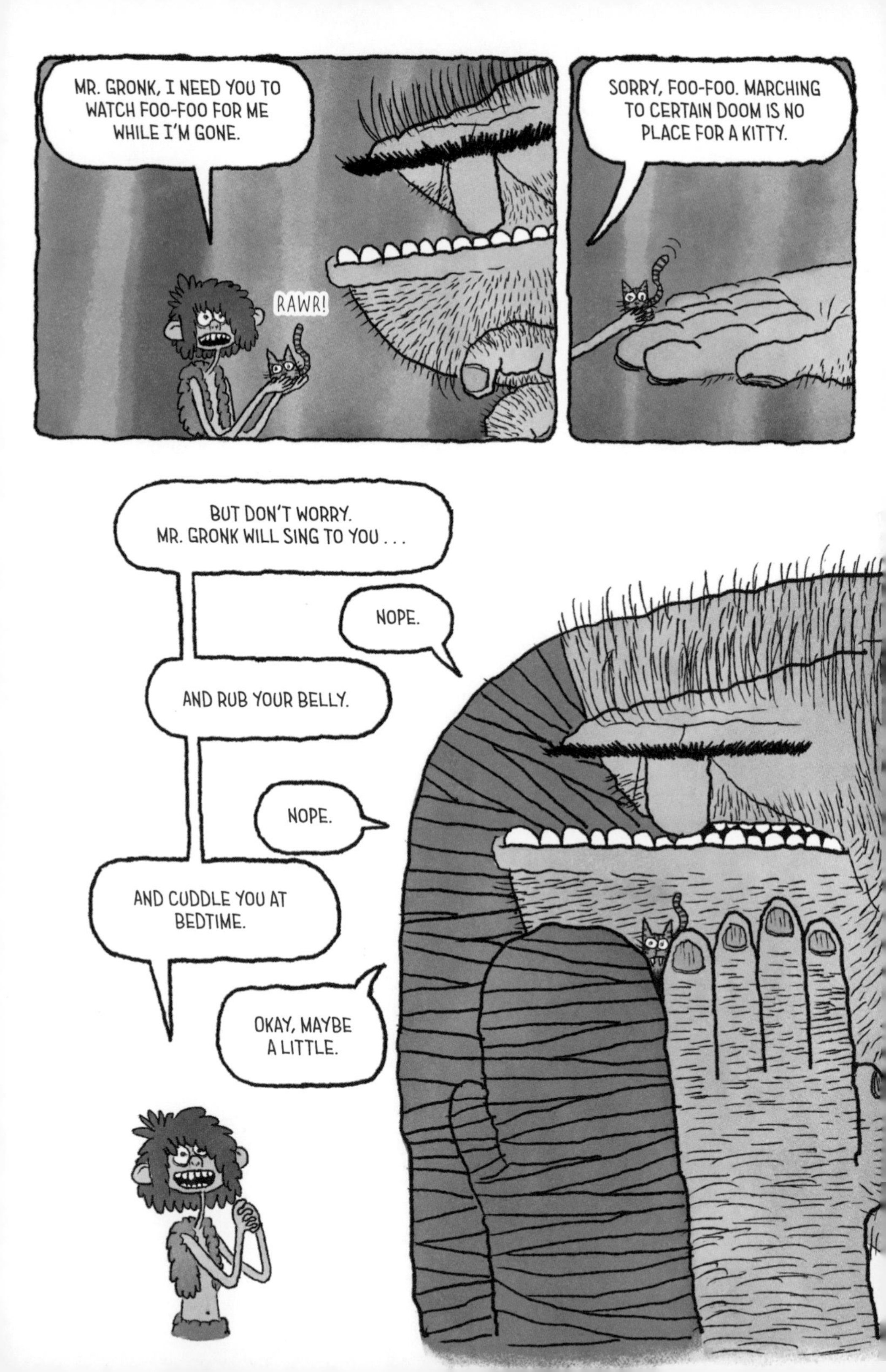
MR. GRONK, I NEED YOU TO WATCH FOO-FOO FOR ME WHILE I'M GONE.
RAWR!
SORRY, FOO-FOO. MARCHING TO CERTAIN DOOM IS NO PLACE FOR A KITTY.
BUT DON'T WORRY. MR. GRONK WILL SING TO YOU . . .
NOPE.
AND RUB YOUR BELLY.
NOPE.
AND CUDDLE YOU AT BEDTIME.
OKAY, MAYBE A LITTLE.

WE'D BETTER GET STARTED.
THE FIELD OF SCREAMS IS A DAY
STRAIGHT NORTH.

I had no idea how this was going to turn out.
LET'S GO HOME, EVERYBODY. THEY'VE GOT THIS UNDER CONTROL.
AND, DAVEY?
YES, MRS. MUKLUK?
But one thing was crystal clear.
TEACH THOSE NO-GOOD, DIRTY, ROTTEN SHAMAN-STEALERS A LESSON.

(GULP) OKAY.
Mrs. Mukluk was terrifying.

7

By the time we got through the forest, there were a few hours of daylight left.
And we were still alive.

But maybe not for long. The stench of brimstone was in the air.
SMELL THAT?
THAT COULD BE ME, BRO. I HAD TAQUITOS FOR LUNCH.
We had arrived at the Field of Screams, a heaving, spurting field of geysers running miles in either direction.

Most geysers just shoot boiling-hot water into the air. No big deal.
But that's not fancy enough for this one. The Field of Screams is sprinkled with five different kinds of geysers.
Roasting red lava.
Scalding blue water.
Molten orange clay.
Scorching black tar.
And blistering green sludge.

It was a minefield of death.
A swamp of sorrows.
A field of screams.
Mostly that's why we call it the Field of Screams.
MY PARENTS USED TO TELL ME HORROR STORIES ABOUT THIS PLACE.
WITH GOOD REASON, LASS. DOZENS OF DEADLY FOUNTAINS SHOOT OFF AT RANDOM EVERY FEW SECONDS.
OUCHIE.
EXACTLY.
DIE.
IT'S LIKE WE'RE SHARING A BRAIN, CLUNK.
LET'S SET UP CAMP.
FOR HOW LONG?
UNTIL WE FIGURE OUT WHAT TO DO NEXT.

Everyone else got settled in, but I couldn't take my eyes off the geysers.
There had to be a way across. If I could only figure it out.
An hour passed.
Two hours.
Three hours.
THREE HOURS OF SITTING AROUND. I CAN'T TAKE THIS ANYMORE.

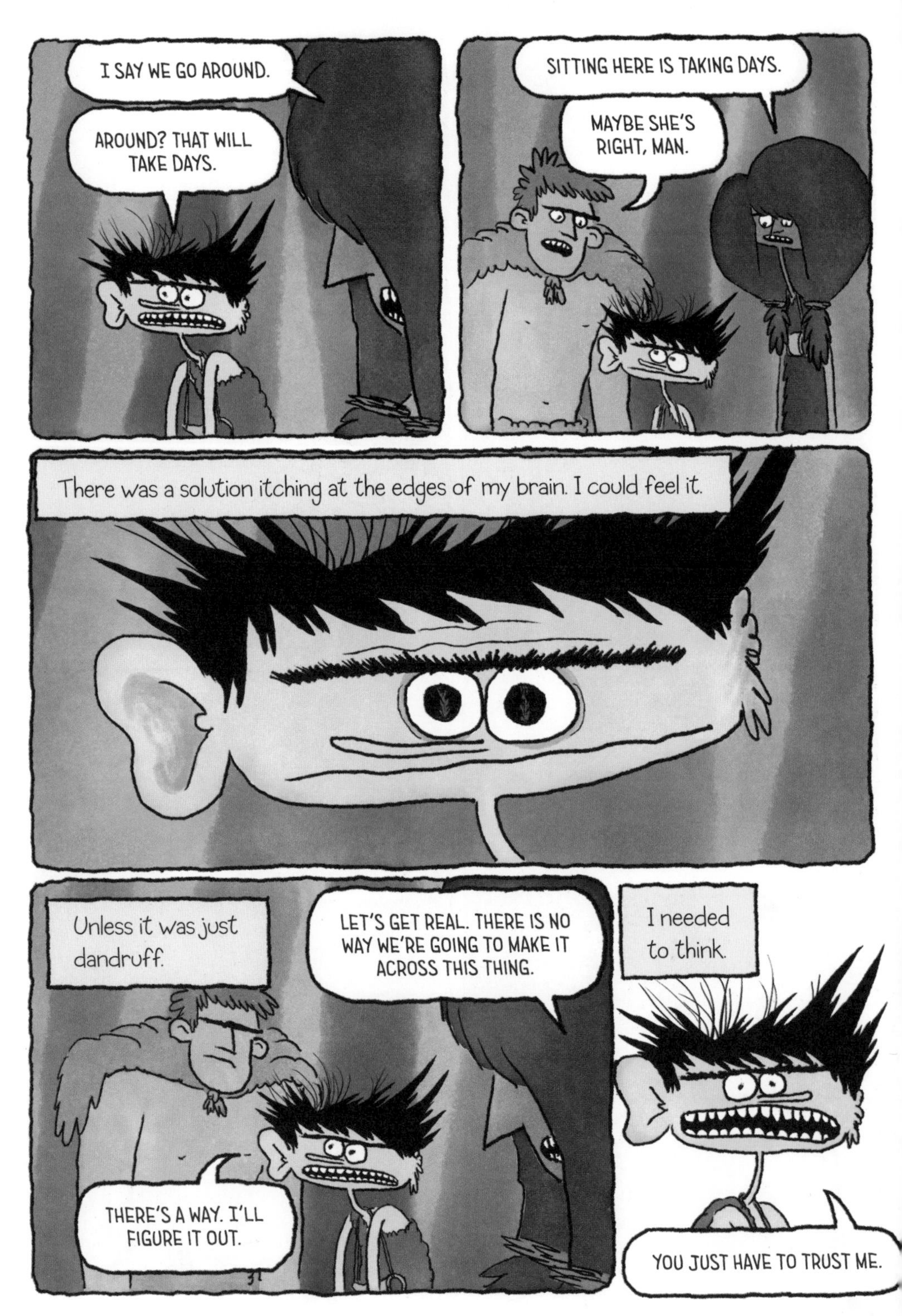
I SAY WE GO AROUND.
AROUND? THAT WILL TAKE DAYS.
SITTING HERE IS TAKING DAYS.
MAYBE SHE'S RIGHT, MAN.
There was a solution itching at the edges of my brain. I could feel it.
Unless it was just dandruff.
LET'S GET REAL. THERE IS NO WAY WE'RE GOING TO MAKE IT ACROSS THIS THING.
THERE'S A WAY. I'LL FIGURE IT OUT.
I needed to think.
YOU JUST HAVE TO TRUST ME.

WE DO, DAVE.
I DON'T KNOW, BIG D. TRUSTING YOU TO GET US ALIVE THROUGH A MINEFIELD OF BURNING HOT GOOP IS ASKING A LOT.
I needed Rockie to quit pressuring me.
HERE'S AN IDEA. WE'LL SPLIT UP AND SOME OF US WILL GO AROUND. WHO'S WITH ME?
NO! WE SHOULD STAY TOGETHER. THIS IS MY DECISION.
YOUR DECISION? LOOK, BOSSYSAUCE, I DON'T WANT YOUR DECISION TO **GET EVERYONE KILLED.**
WILL YOU STOP? YOU ARE HERE TO SUPPORT ME AND ADVISE ME. NOT TAKE OVER!
I *AM* ADVISING YOU, IF YOU'D USE THOSE EARS CONNECTED TO THAT BIG BRAIN OF YOURS!
NO, YOU AREN'T. YOU KEEP QUESTIONING EVERY DECISION I MAKE!

LET'S BE HONEST—THE WAY YOU HANDLED MR. STONEWALL AND THE LIZARD BROTHERS WASN'T EXACTLY STELLAR.
HEY!
AND THIS BRILLIANT RESCUE PLAN ISN'T WORKING OUT SO STELLAR, EITHER. I TOLD YOU IT WASN'T A SMART IDEA.
THAT'S ENOUGH!
WELL, I'M NOT JUST GOING TO TELL YOU WHAT YOU WANT TO HEAR. ESPECIALLY WHEN **YOU'RE WRONG!**
Leave it to Rockie to keep me on my toes.
NO, YOU'RE GOING TO MAKE THE DECISION YOURSELF AND MAKE ME LOOK LIKE AN IDIOT!
OH, YOU DON'T NEED ANY HELP FROM ME ON THAT.
OH, REALLY?
LOOK, DAVE. I DIDN'T MEAN . . .

YOU'RE ABSOLUTELY RIGHT. I DON'T NEED ANY HELP FROM YOU!
WHAT'S THAT SUPPOSED TO MEAN?
I CAN'T GET RID OF MY DAD. THE VILLAGE PICKED HIM.
WHY DRAG *ME* INTO THIS? I'M MR. SUPPORTIVE!
BUT I CAN GET RID OF YOU. **YOU'RE FIRED, ROCKIE!**
WHAT?
FIRED!

I NEED SOMEBODY WHO'S GOING TO LISTEN TO ME.
YOU MEAN SOMEBODY WHO WILL DO WHAT YOU SAY?
SOMEBODY WHO TRUSTS ME.
YOU MEAN SOMEBODY WHO CAN'T THINK FOR THEMSELVES?
SOMEBODY WHO . . .
SOMEBODY WHO WON'T QUESTION YOU WHEN YOU'RE ABOUT TO CRASH AND BURN?
MAYBE THAT'S **EXACTLY** WHAT I NEED!
HEY, UG?
YEAH?
YOU'RE MY NEW ADVISER.
WOW, DAVE . . . IT'S A SUPER-CUTE NECKLACE AND ALL, BUT I'M NOT SURE . . .

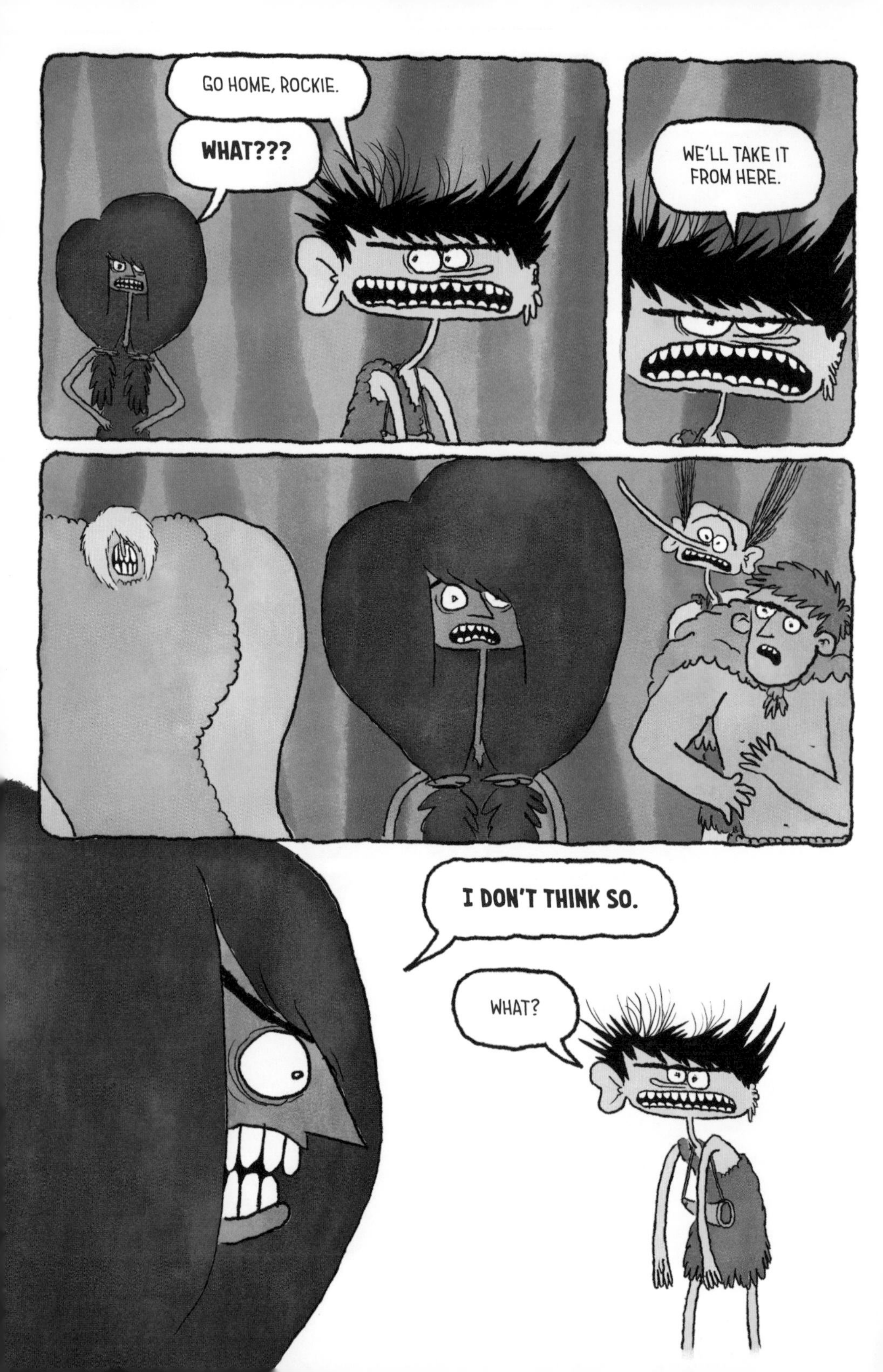
GO HOME, ROCKIE.
WHAT???
WE'LL TAKE IT FROM HERE.
I DON'T THINK SO.
WHAT?

YOU HEARD ME. YOU CAN FIRE ME. BUT YOU CAN'T MAKE ME RUN HOME.
BESIDES . . . YOU'RE GOING TO BE BEGGING FOR MY HELP BEFORE THIS IS ALL FINISHED.
FAT CHANCE. I WOULDN'T ASK FOR YOUR HELP IF MY LIFE DEPENDED ON IT.
FINE!
FINE!
JUST ONE THING, DAVE.
YEAH?

I DON'T REALLY KNOW
WHAT AN ADVISER IS.
SO YOU'RE GOING TO HAVE TO
TELL ME WHAT TO DO.
Yep. This new arrangement was going to work out just fine.

8

There was no time to decide how I felt about what just happened.
THAT'S IT! I CAN'T TAKE THIS TENSION!

I'M JUST MAKING A RUN FOR IT! IF WE RUN FAST ENOUGH, WE'LL MAKE IT ACROSS!
SEE YOU ON THE OTHER SIDE, SUCKERS!
BAD IDEA. EVEN CLUNK KNOW THAT.

HAVE YOU LOST YOUR MIND, BANE? DID YOU SEE MR. GRONK'S ARM?
AND DON'T FORGET CRISPY JIM.
SMELLS LIKE SOMEBODY'S BISCUITS ARE BURNING!
WELL, ROCKIE'S RIGHT ABOUT ONE THING. WE NEED TO DO SOMETHING!
RELAX, BRO. GAZE AT THE TRANQUIL PATTERNS OF COLOR. IT'S REALLY QUITE ZEN.

And that's when it hit me.
SAY THAT AGAIN, UG!
TRANQUIL PATTERNS OF COLOR, BRO.
PATTERNS! UG, YOU'RE A GENIUS!
AFFIRMATIVE, BRO.
RED! GREEN! ORANGE! BLACK! BLACK! BLUE! GREEN! ORANGE!
WHAT ARE YOU GIBBERING ABOUT, BOY? HAS THE PRESSURE MADE YOU GO WOBBLY IN THE NOGGIN?
WE ALWAYS ASSUMED THE SPURTS WERE RANDOM!
LOOKS PRETTY RANDOM TO ME.

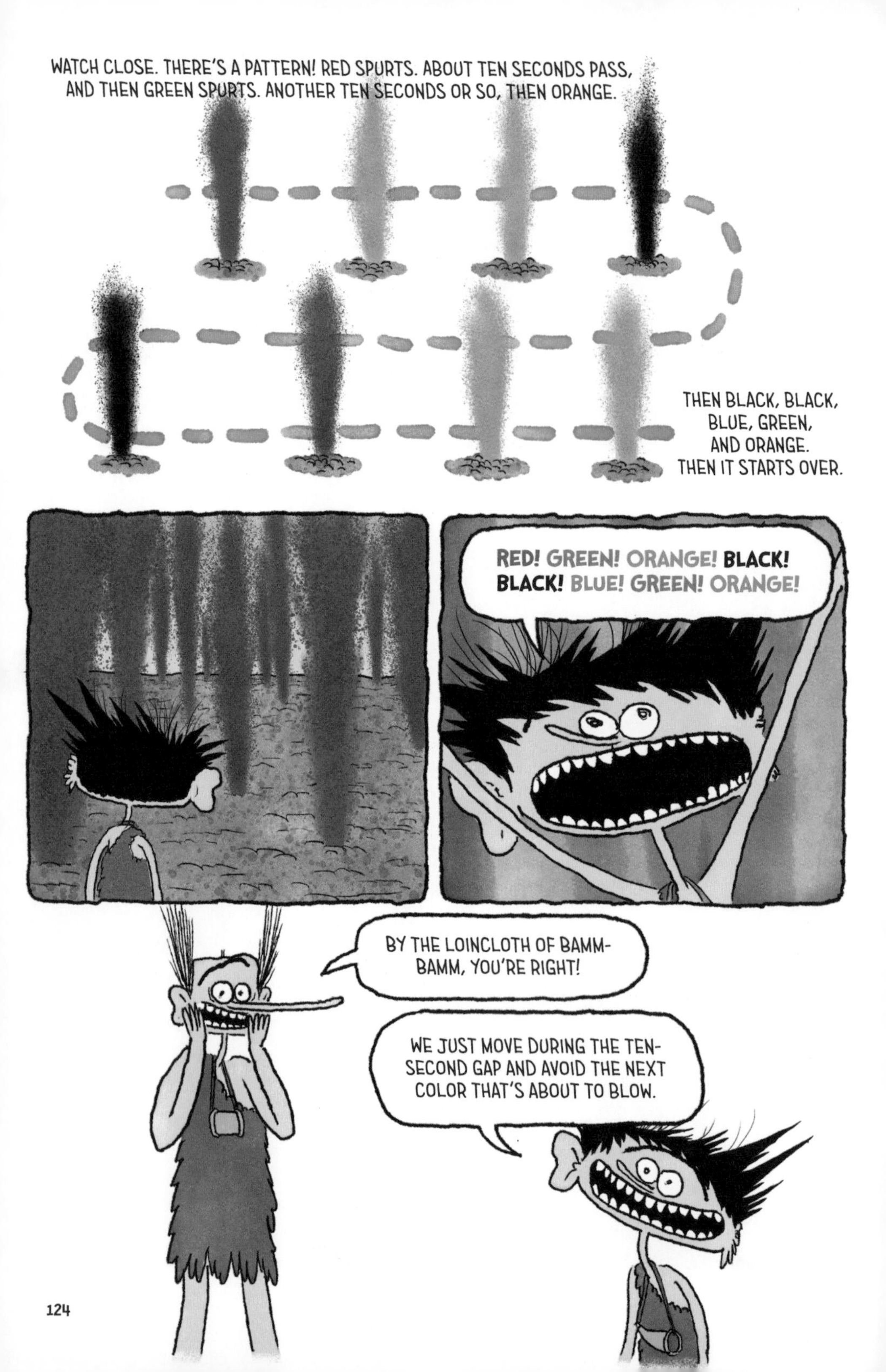
WATCH CLOSE. THERE'S A PATTERN! RED SPURTS. ABOUT TEN SECONDS PASS, AND THEN GREEN SPURTS. ANOTHER TEN SECONDS OR SO, THEN ORANGE.
THEN BLACK, BLACK, BLUE, GREEN, AND ORANGE. THEN IT STARTS OVER.
RED! GREEN! ORANGE! BLACK! BLACK! BLUE! GREEN! ORANGE!
BY THE LOINCLOTH OF BAMM-BAMM, YOU'RE RIGHT!
WE JUST MOVE DURING THE TEN-SECOND GAP AND AVOID THE NEXT COLOR THAT'S ABOUT TO BLOW.

I CAN'T DO IT! I CAN'T REMEMBER ALL THOSE COLORS!
BLUE! PURPLE! TURQUOISE! TRIANGLE!
THAT'S A SHAPE, BRO. NOT A COLOR.
RELAX, BANE. I'LL GO FIRST.
IF I'M RIGHT, THEN I'LL CALL OUT THE COLOR THAT WILL SHOOT NEXT AND THE REST OF YOU CAN GO ONE AT A TIME.
SON, LET ME GO WITH YOU. . . .
NO, DAD.
BOY, LISTEN . . .
STOP IT, DAD!

YOU CAN'T PROTECT ME FROM EVERYTHING.
I CAN TRY!
DAD, MR. GRONK ALREADY GOT BURNED. I DON'T WANT ANYONE ELSE GETTING HURT BECAUSE OF ME.
BUT . . .
JUST STAND HERE WITH ME, MR. UNGA-BUNGA. LET MR. WONDERFUL WORK HIS MAGIC.
I stepped up to the edge. I took a deep breath.
JUST ONE IMPORTANT TIP, BRO. DON'T DIE.
GOT IT.
And I crossed.

RED!
GREEN!
ORANGE!
WHOA!
FASTER, MAN! PUT A LITTLE BOOGIE IN IT!
BLACK! BLACK!
BLUE! GREEN!
ORANGE!

I couldn't believe it. I was on the other side. And I was alive.
THAT LITTLE GUY HAS THE BIGGEST GUTS I KNOW.
YEAH, AND HE'S GOT AN EVEN BIGGER HEAD.
So, one by one, we crossed. . . . I shouted out colors from the other side.
RED! GREEN!
And other words of encouragement.
TRIANGLE!!!
QUIT RUSHING, YOU IDIOT!

Of course, some of us knew everything and weren't getting any help from me.
ORANGE! BLACK! BLACK! BLUE!
But one by one, we did what nobody had ever done.
GREEN! ORANGE!
Except Crispy Jim.
DOES ANYONE ELSE TASTE SOOT?

As the last rays of sunlight were fading,
we all made it across the Field of Screams.

BRO! THAT WAS BRILLIANT.
IT WASN'T JUST BRILLIANT. IT WAS AMAZING!
OH, BOY.
I GUESS I REALLY AM AS AWESOME AS THE VILLAGE THINKS I AM!
OH, BOY.
NOW THAT I THINK ABOUT IT, WHY HAVEN'T THEY PUT ME IN CHARGE BEFORE NOW?
OH, BOY.
SOMEBODY TELL HIS ROYAL AWESOMENESS NOT TO GET AHEAD OF HIMSELF.
DAVE, ROCKIE SAYS NOT TO GET AHEAD OF YOURSELF.
I'M SORRY. WHO? I DON'T KNOW ANY "ROCKIE."

ROCKIE, HE DOESN'T SEEM TO KNOW WHO YOU ARE. IT'S REALLY BIZARRE.
WHATEVER. BUT WE'RE NOT COMPLETELY SAFE JUST YET.
WHAT DO YOU MEAN?
LOOK. FIRELIGHT.
LOOK, EVERYONE. FIRELIGHT.
THERE'S SOMETHING WEIRD ABOUT THAT FIRELIGHT. I CAN'T PUT MY FINGER ON IT.
IT'S NOT ON THE GROUND. . . .
LOOK, EVERYONE, IT'S NOT ON THE GROUND.
KNOCK THAT OFF! I KNOW YOU CAN HEAR ME!

THEY LIVE IN THE TREES.
THAT'S CRAZY.
I KNOW! HAVING A FIRE IN A TREE? THAT'S THE FIRST RULE OF FIRE SAFETY: "DON'T HAVE A FIRE IN A TREE."
BUT WHERE ARE THE PEOPLE?
SHH! I HEAR VOICES.
YOU HAD TO ASK, BRO. WHY DO YOU ALWAYS HAVE TO ASK?

ARE . . .
ARE THOSE . . .
BIRDS?
SHH!
THAT EXPLAINS WHY THEY LIVE IN TREES. THEY'RE NOT HUMAN. THEY'RE . . .
BIRD-PEOPLE.
DOESN'T MATTER, BRO. IF THEY HEAR US, WE'RE ALL GOING TO BE DEAD DUCKS.
HE'S RIGHT. LET'S FIND SHAMAN FABOO BEFORE THESE FEATHERED WEIRDOS FIND US.

WAIT!
KEEP GOING!
NO, WAIT!
NO, KEEP GOING!
CLUNK CONFUSED. WAIT OR KEEP GOING?
CAN'T WE ALL JUST GET ALONG? ALL THIS TENSION IS GIVING ME INTESTINAL DISTRESS.

I MEAN IT! STOP AND LOOK! IN THAT HUT.
YOU MEAN THAT ONE THAT'S TOTALLY DARK INSIDE?
THAT ONE THAT'S SO SHROUDED IN SHADOWS THAT YOU CAN'T MAKE OUT ANYTHING INSIDE?
LOOK IN THAT ONE?
YES. LOOK!
THAT'S SHAMAN FABOO'S STAFF.
LOOKS LIKE A STICK-SHAPED BLOB TO ME.

I HATE TO ADMIT IT, LASS, BUT HE'S RIGHT. THAT COULD BE ANYTHING.
NO, IT COULDN'T. MY PARENTS CARVED TWO OF THOSE STAFFS FOR THE SHAMAN YEARS AGO. I'D KNOW MY PARENTS' WORK ANYWHERE.
IF YOU'RE RIGHT, THAT MEANS SHAMAN FABOO IS IN THAT HUT.
OKAY . . . WE BARGE IN THERE, GRAB SHAMAN FABOO, AND GET AWAY BEFORE THEY EVER KNEW WE WERE HERE.
LET'S NOT BE RASH, BOY. THERE COULD BE OTHERS AROUND. MAYBE WE SHOULD SPLIT UP. . . .
NO! THAT'S EXACTLY WHAT ROCKIE WANTED US TO DO BEFORE!
HE REMEMBERED WHO ROCKIE IS!
NO, I DID NOT!
FALSE ALARM, AMIGOS. HE STILL HAS ROCKIE-SPECIFIC MEMORY LOSS.
MAYBE SHE WAS RIGHT, LAD. SPLITTING UP ISN'T THE WORST IDEA. . . .
NO! SHE WASN'T RIGHT THEN AND YOU'RE NOT RIGHT NOW! JUST TRUST ME!
SHEESH, WE DO, DORK. BUT HOW ARE WE SUPPOSED TO GET UP TO THAT HUT WITHOUT BEING SEEN?

YEAH, MAN. IT'S LIKE THIRTY FEET IN THE AIR.
DON'T WORRY. I'VE ALREADY INVENTED THE SOLUTION TO THAT.

9

REMEMBER THAT TIME YOU INVENTED UNDERWEAR?

WELL, THIS IS CRAZIER THAN UNDERWEAR.
SHHHHHH!
KEEP QUIET, AND STAY NEAR THE TREES.
SOMEONE'S COMING!

SEE? EASY-SQUEEZY.
EVERYBODY QUIETLY UNTIE YOUR STILTS. WE'LL LEAVE THEM HERE.

HEY, DAVE?
YOU CAN IGNORE ME ALL YOU WANT, BUT I'M STILL GOING TO SAY WHAT I NEED TO SAY.
I LOST MY MOM WHEN I WAS YOUNGER. JUST LIKE YOU DID.
MY DAD, TOO. I WAS ABOUT SEVEN WHEN IT HAPPENED.

THEY WERE TEACHING ME TO BE A CARVER. THEY EVEN NAMED ME CARVER. YOU DIDN'T KNOW THAT USED TO BE MY NAME, DID YOU?
WHENEVER WE WORKED, MY DAD WOULD POINT OUT WHAT I WAS DOING WRONG TO TRY TO HELP ME.
"HOLD YOUR CARVING STONE LIKE THIS." "CARVE WITH THE GRAIN, NOT AGAINST IT." I KNEW HE WAS JUST TRYING TO HELP ME GET BETTER, BUT IT DROVE ME CRAZY.
I STOPPED CARVING COMPLETELY WHEN THEY DIED. IT DIDN'T SEEM RIGHT DOING IT WITHOUT HIM THERE TELLING ME WHAT TO DO.
I EVEN STOPPED GOING BY THE NAME CARVER. EVERY TIME I HEARD IT, I THOUGHT OF THEM. I COULDN'T HANDLE THAT.

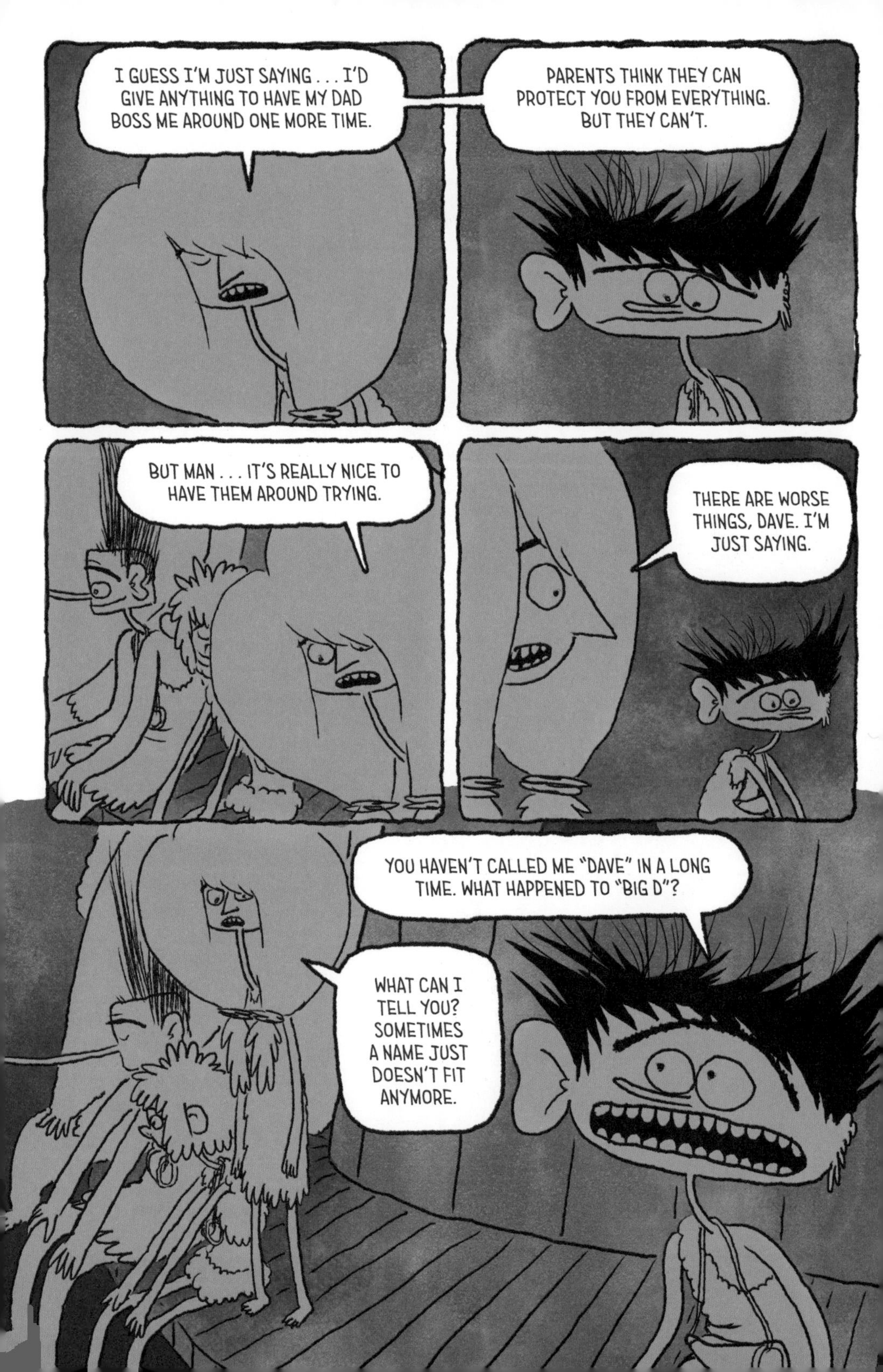
I GUESS I'M JUST SAYING . . . I'D GIVE ANYTHING TO HAVE MY DAD BOSS ME AROUND ONE MORE TIME.
PARENTS THINK THEY CAN PROTECT YOU FROM EVERYTHING. BUT THEY CAN'T.
BUT MAN . . . IT'S REALLY NICE TO HAVE THEM AROUND TRYING.
THERE ARE WORSE THINGS, DAVE. I'M JUST SAYING.
YOU HAVEN'T CALLED ME "DAVE" IN A LONG TIME. WHAT HAPPENED TO "BIG D"?
WHAT CAN I TELL YOU? SOMETIMES A NAME JUST DOESN'T FIT ANYMORE.

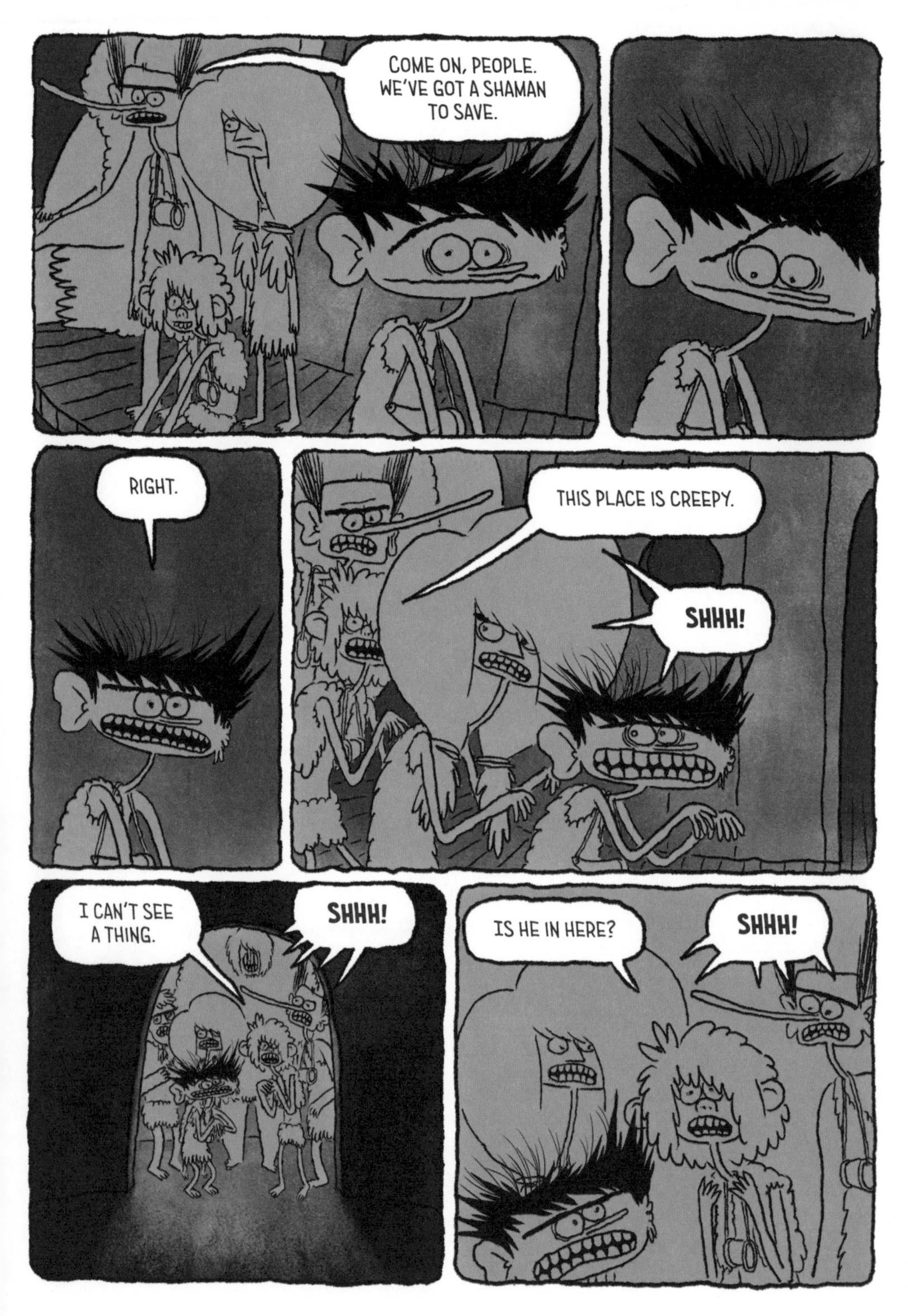
COME ON, PEOPLE. WE'VE GOT A SHAMAN TO SAVE.
RIGHT.
THIS PLACE IS CREEPY.
SHHH!
I CAN'T SEE A THING.
SHHH!
IS HE IN HERE?
SHHH!

SHAMAN! WE'RE HERE TO RESCUE YOU.
BUT . . .
DON'T TALK, SHAMAN! THESE GUYS WILL ONLY SHUSH YOU.
WE'LL HAVE YOU OUT OF HERE AND SAFE BACK HOME IN NO TIME.
LET'S GO!
SEE? EASY-SQUEEZY.

PUT YOUR NECK IN MY FIST, DAVE. I'LL SHOW YOU EASY-SQUEEZY.
WHAT DO WE DO? WHAT DO WE DO?
UP.

I DON'T THINK THAT'S SUCH A GOOD IDEA, DAVE.
UP!
WE'RE GOING TO BE TRAPPED IF WE GO UP THERE!
THEY'RE COMING! THE BIRDIES ARE COMING!
KEEP GOING!
BRO, I'M PRETTY GO-WITH-THE-FLOW, BUT I'M NOT SURE I LIKE WHERE THIS IS FLOWING.
DEAD END!

BIRDY! TWEET, TWEET, BIRDY!
BANE SAY TWEET TWEET.
HE'S SNAPPED, SISTER. THE DUDE DOES NOT LIKE BIRDS.
NOW WHAT?
EVERYBODY HOLD ON TO ME!
WHAT?
DO IT!

WELL, THIS IS A TOUCHING MOMENT AND ALL, BUT OUR SITUATION HAS NOT IMPROVED.
HOLD ON TIGHT!
AAAAAAHHHHHHHHH!
BIRDY GO FLY-FLY!
EXACTLY.

FLICK

CREAK
MAX CAPACITY
10 PEOPLE
UH-OH.

OW.

10

EVERYBODY OKAY?
SWEET RIDE, BRO. SWEET RIDE.
WHOA. WHAT HAPPENED?
YOU TOTALLY SNAPPED, MAN.
NO MORE BIRDS, MAN. THAT FREAKED ME OUT.

FIFTY BIRD-PEOPLE CLOSING IN IS ENOUGH TO MAKE ANYONE GO A LITTLE PEE-PEE IN THEIR LOINCLOTH.
I NEVER SAID I WENT PEE-PEE.
YOU DIDN'T HAVE TO, BRO. THE NOSE KNOWS.
THE IMPORTANT THING IS WE LOST THEM.
AND LOOK! YOU MANAGED TO FLY THROUGH THE AIR, WEE-WEE A LITTLE, AND STILL HOLD ON TO SHAMAN FABOO.
THERE WAS NO WEE-WEE INVOLVED.

BANE, SET THE SHAMAN DOWN.
WHOA! THEY TURNED SHAMAN FABOO INTO ONE OF THOSE WEIRD BIRD-PEOPLE!
AHHH! BIRD-PERSON!
EVERYBODY STOP GOING AHHH!

LOOK! IT'S NOT A BIRD-PERSON.
YOU'RE RIGHT, LAD. IT'S JUST SOME SORT OF BEAKY FEATHERY HEADDRESS.
THEY ALL MUST HAVE BEEN WEARING THEM.
WHICH MEANS THEY'RE NOT BIRD-PEOPLE. THEY'RE JUST PEOPLE. LIKE US.
BUT, BRO. WHY WOULD THEY WEAR FEATHERS AND BIRD MASKS?
YEAH. AND WHY WOULD THEY PUT ONE ON SHAMAN FABOO?

AHHH! NOT SHAMAN FABOO!
WHO ARE YOU, LADY?
I'M SHAMAN EMBER.
SHAMAN WHAT-NOW?
SHAMAN EMBER.

WHAT HAVE YOU DONE WITH SHAMAN FABOO?!
NOTHING AT ALL. WHAT HAS HAPPENED TO FABOO?
YOU TOOK HIM!
I CAN ASSURE YOU, I DID NOT.
BUT YOU HAVE HIS STAFF.
THIS IS NOT HIS STAFF.
I KNOW MY PARENTS' CARVING WHEN I SEE IT!
TWO WERE CARVED, I BELIEVE?
HOW DID YOU KNOW THAT?
FABOO KEPT ONE. AND HE GAVE THE OTHER ONE TO ME. MANY YEARS AGO.

YOU KNOW SHAMAN FABOO?
YES. WE WERE . . . CLOSE FRIENDS BACK IN SHAMAN SCHOOL.
SHAMAN SCHOOL? THERE'S SHAMAN SCHOOL? I'VE JUST BEEN WINGING IT!
TRUST ME, DAVE. THERE'S NOT ENOUGH SCHOOL IN THE WORLD TO MAKE YOU A BETTER SHAMAN.
YOWTCH! LET ME FIND YOU SOME ALOE VERA, DAVE! 'CAUSE YOU JUST GOT BURNED!
NO, I DIDN'T!
WHOA, SPEAKING OF BURNS . . .
I DIDN'T GET BURNED!
IF YOU WEREN'T BURNING THAT BONFIRE TO CELEBRATE CAPTURING SHAMAN FABOO, THEN HOW COME YOU WERE BURNING IT?
MY DEAR BOY, WE ALWAYS BURN IT. IT'S THE ONLY THING THAT KEEPS THE RIPPY-BEAKS AT BAY.

BALANCING BOULDERS.
WHAT?
THE FIRE HAS ALWAYS BEEN BURNING. WE COULDN'T SEE THE SMOKE BECAUSE BALANCING BOULDERS BLOCKED OUR VIEW.
YOU SEE, OUR VILLAGE HAS LONG BEEN PLAGUED BY A FEROCIOUS FLOCK OF RIPPY-BEAKS. LED BY ONE HUGE SPECIMEN IN PARTICULAR.
THAT BIG ONE WE SAW.
THE ONE THAT CAUGHT THE POKEYHORN.
THE FIRE KEEPS THE CREATURES AT SOME DISTANCE. THAT AND WEARING THE FEATHERS AND MASKS.

THE RIPPY-BEAKS THINK YOU ARE BIRDS. SO THEY LEAVE YOU ALONE.
PRECISELY.
BUT WHEN ROCKSTACK PYRE FELL MANY DAYS AGO . . .
YOU MEAN BALANCING BOULDERS.
YOU MEAN GEORGE.
WHEN THE LARGE STACK OF BOULDERS FELL . . . THE RIPPY-BEAKS DISAPPEARED.
PERHAPS THEY WERE CRUSHED. PERHAPS THEY WERE SCARED OFF.
SO YOU DIDN'T NEED THE FIRE ANYMORE.
THAT IS CORRECT.

OH MY GOSH.
THEY NEVER TOOK SHAMAN FABOO IN THE FIRST PLACE.
YOU SAY THAT MY DEAR FRIEND FABOO IS IN DANGER?
HE'S GONE MISSING.
WE THOUGHT YOU KIDNAPPED HIM.
AN ILL-CONCEIVED NOTION.
IF THAT MEANS DAVE WAS COMPLETELY WRONG, THEN YEAH.
WE NEED TO GET YOU BACK TO YOUR VILLAGE. BEFORE THEY COME AFTER US.
DO NOT WORRY. IT WAS A SIMPLE MISUNDERSTANDING. I WILL MAKE THEM SEE.

HOLD ON JUST A SHAMAN-STEALING MINUTE. WHAT IF SHE'S LYING?
DAVE . . .
I TOLD THE VILLAGE WE WOULD BRING BACK SHAMAN FABOO. AND THAT'S WHAT WE'RE GOING TO DO.
LOOK, BOY . . .
WE HANG ON TO HER. THEN IF THEY DO HAVE SHAMAN FABOO, WE CAN SWAP HER.
LET ME GET THIS STRAIGHT, DINGBAT. ARE YOU SAYING WE SHOULD HOLD SHAMAN EMBER **HOSTAGE?**
WHAT IF I AM?
YOU HAVE FINALLY LOST YOUR MIND.

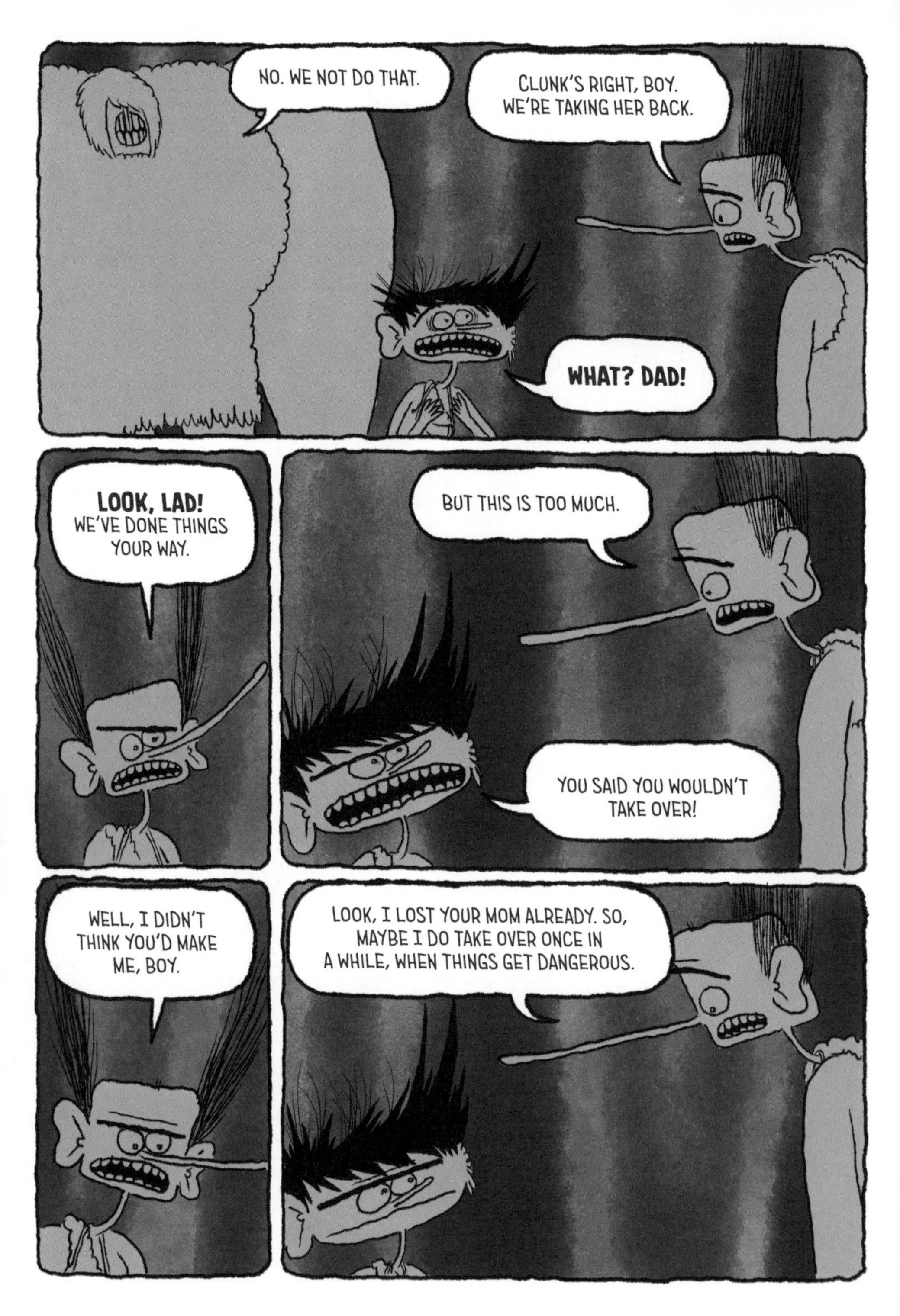
NO. WE NOT DO THAT.
CLUNK'S RIGHT, BOY. WE'RE TAKING HER BACK.
WHAT? DAD!
LOOK, LAD! WE'VE DONE THINGS YOUR WAY.
BUT THIS IS TOO MUCH.
YOU SAID YOU WOULDN'T TAKE OVER!
WELL, I DIDN'T THINK YOU'D MAKE ME, BOY.
LOOK, I LOST YOUR MOM ALREADY. SO, MAYBE I DO TAKE OVER ONCE IN A WHILE, WHEN THINGS GET DANGEROUS.

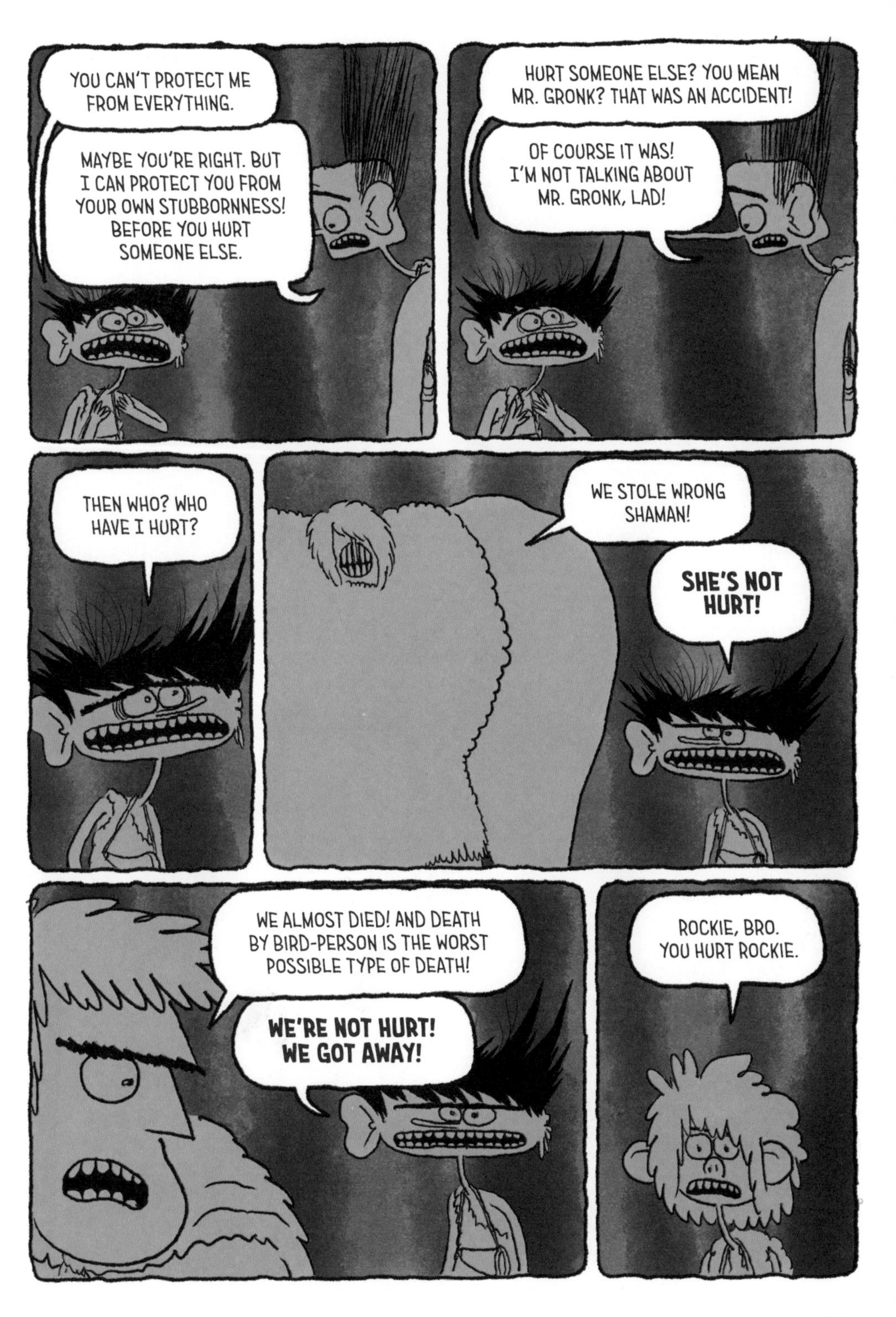
YOU CAN'T PROTECT ME FROM EVERYTHING.
MAYBE YOU'RE RIGHT. BUT I CAN PROTECT YOU FROM YOUR OWN STUBBORNNESS! BEFORE YOU HURT SOMEONE ELSE.
HURT SOMEONE ELSE? YOU MEAN MR. GRONK? THAT WAS AN ACCIDENT!
OF COURSE IT WAS! I'M NOT TALKING ABOUT MR. GRONK, LAD!
THEN WHO? WHO HAVE I HURT?
WE STOLE WRONG SHAMAN!
SHE'S NOT HURT!
WE ALMOST DIED! AND DEATH BY BIRD-PERSON IS THE WORST POSSIBLE TYPE OF DEATH!
WE'RE NOT HURT! WE GOT AWAY!
ROCKIE, BRO. YOU HURT ROCKIE.

WELL . . . SHE WOULDN'T LISTEN!
YOU WON'T LISTEN, BOSSY BRITCHES!
WHAT ARE BRITCHES?
NO IDEA.
YOU'RE TRYING SO HARD TO BE THE BOSS, YOU'RE FORGETTING TO JUST BE DAVE!
THE DAVE I KNOW IS GREAT AT THINKING ON HIS FEET.
IT'S TRUE, DORK. YOU ALWAYS COME UP WITH THESE GREAT IDEAS WHEN NOBODY KNOWS WHAT TO DO.

BUT YOU USED TO LISTEN, TOO, BRO.
USED TO?
SORRY, MAN. YOU KINDA STOPPED BEING THAT GUY A WHILE AGO.
BUT YOU SAID THE WHOLE THING ABOUT THE STICK!
WHAT?
THAT IF I'M THROWING THE STICK AND EVERYONE FOLLOWS IT, THEN I'M THE LEADER!
LOOK AROUND, LAD! NOBODY'S FOLLOWING YOUR STICK!
INCLUDING ME. SORRY, BOY.

I'M TAKING SHAMAN EMBER BACK TO HER PEOPLE.
GREAT! THIS IS WHAT I GET FOR STEPPING UP WHEN NO ONE ELSE WOULD!
THIS IS WHAT I GET FOR TRYING TO HELP!
THIS IS WHAT I GET FOR STICKING MY NECK OUT!

OH, CRAP.
OH, CRAP.
OH, CRAP.

OH, CRAP.

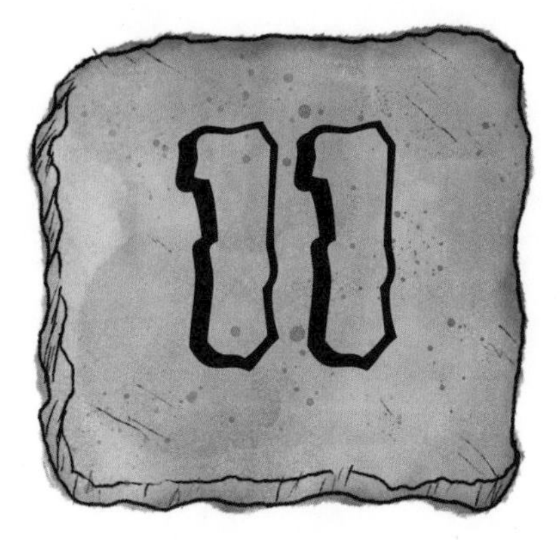
11

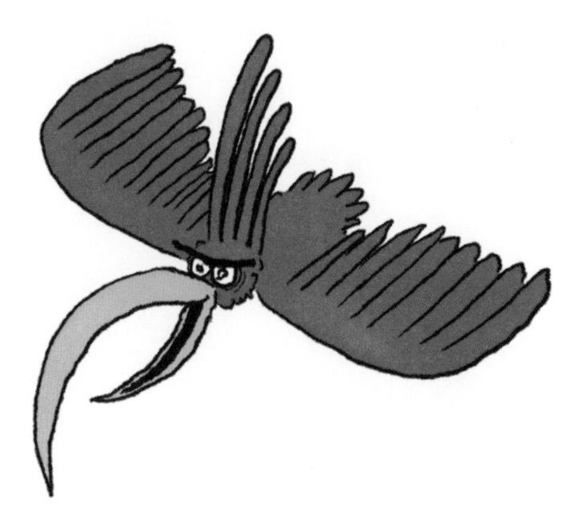

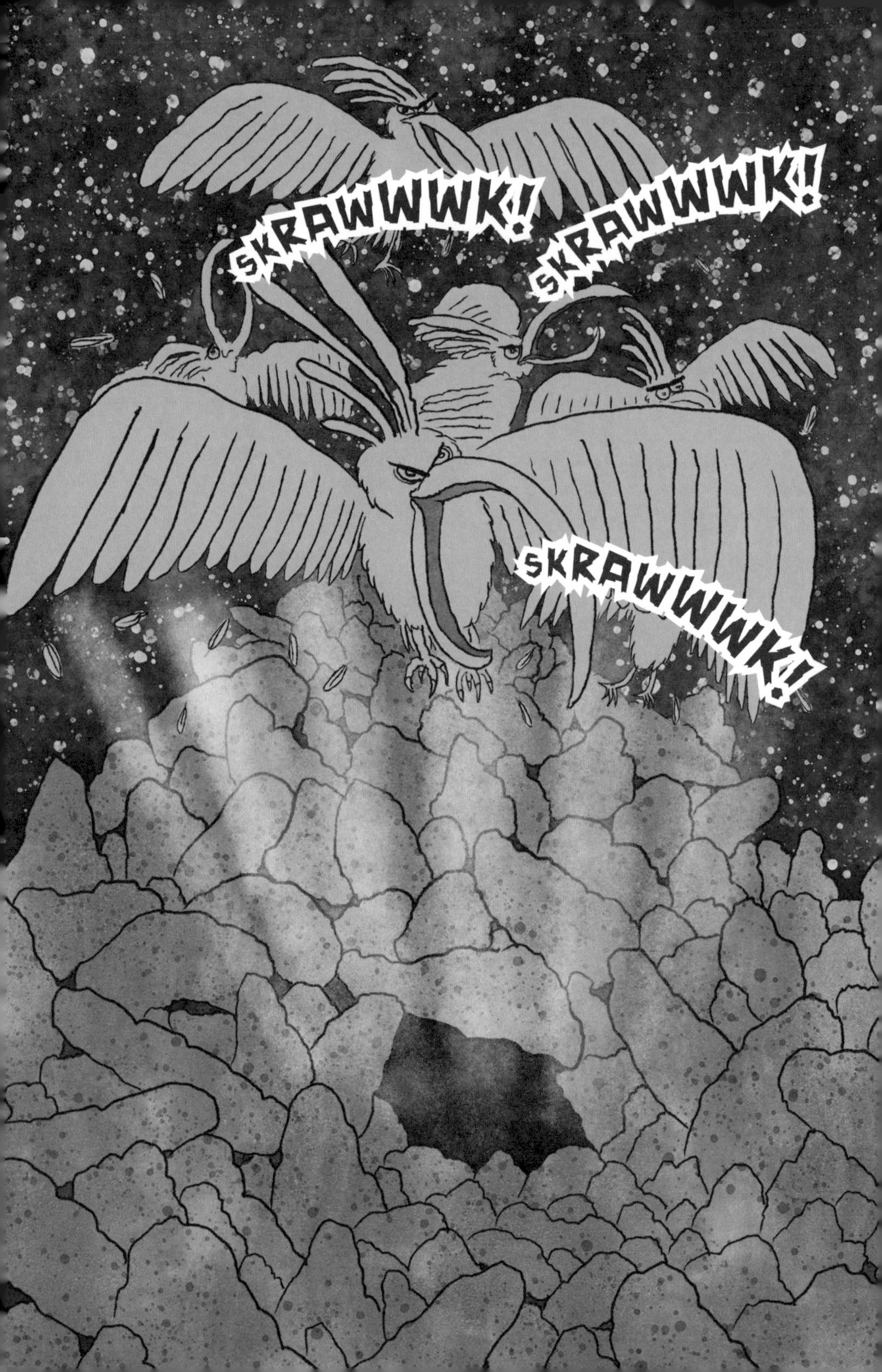
SKRAWWWK!
SKRAWWWK!
SKRAWWWK!

WE'RE DEAD! YOU'VE OFFICIALLY MADE US DEAD!
R.I.P. TO US, BRO. WE CAN'T OUTRUN THOSE THINGS!
IT MATTERS NOT! THE FIRE IS OUT. THEY ARE HEADING TO MY VILLAGE!
WITHOUT THE BONFIRE BURNING, NOT EVEN OUR DISGUISES WILL KEEP THE FLYING BEASTS FROM ATTACKING!

LADY, WAIT!
MY PEOPLE ARE COUNTING ON ME!
YOU CAN'T DO ANYTHING ABOUT IT BY YOURSELF!
YOU ARE RIGHT. I CANNOT FIX THIS.
BUT A SHAMAN CAN SIMPLY BE THERE FOR HER PEOPLE.
EVEN UNTO DEATH.
MAYBE YOU DON'T HAVE TO GO, LIKE . . . UNTO DEATH.
I THINK . . . MAYBE . . . I HAVE AN IDEA.
YOU?
YOU?
YOU?
I KNOW, RIGHT?
I'M LISTENING, STRANGE ONE.

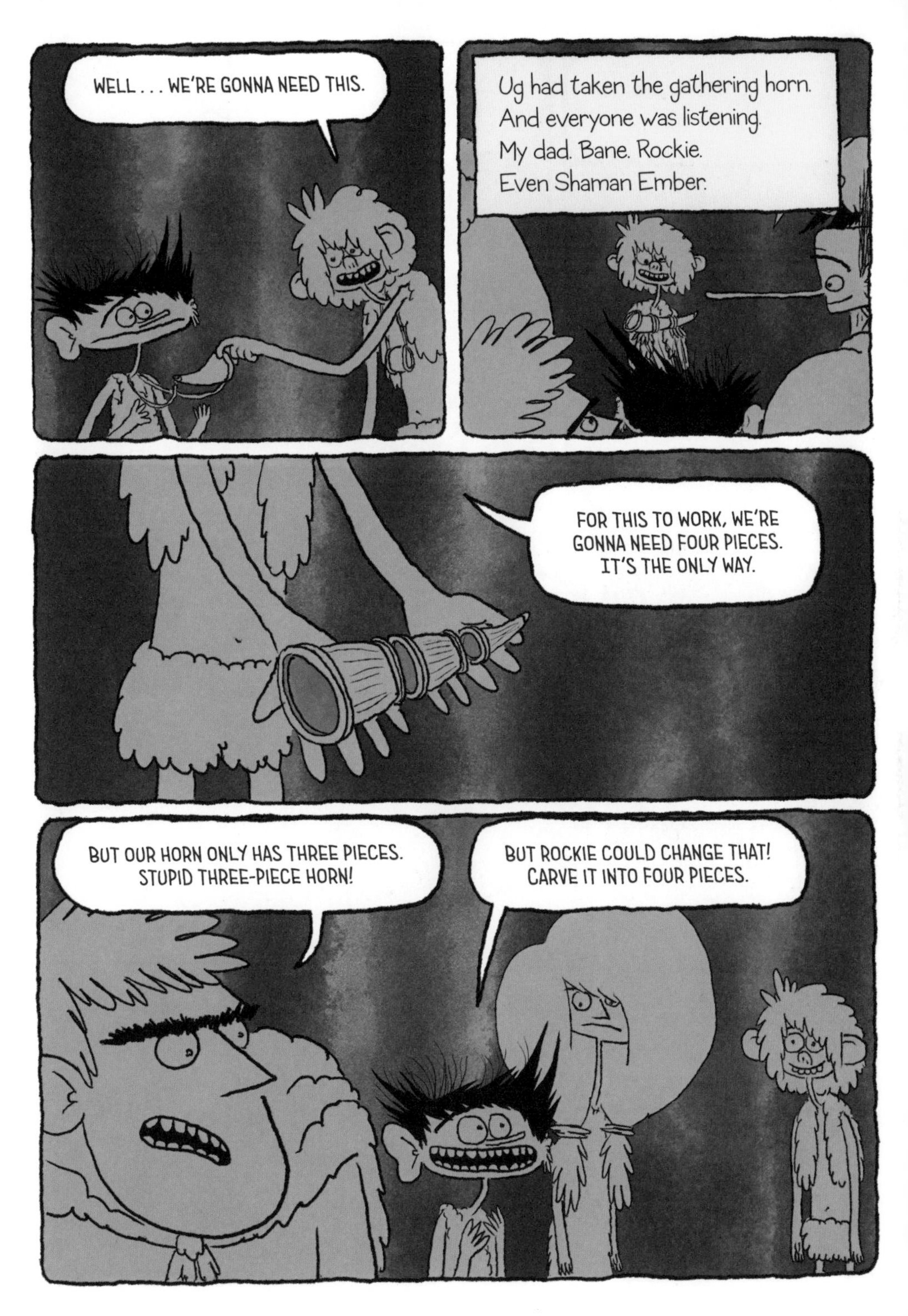
WELL . . . WE'RE GONNA NEED THIS.
Ug had taken the gathering horn.
And everyone was listening.
My dad. Bane. Rockie.
Even Shaman Ember.
FOR THIS TO WORK, WE'RE GONNA NEED FOUR PIECES. IT'S THE ONLY WAY.
BUT OUR HORN ONLY HAS THREE PIECES. STUPID THREE-PIECE HORN!
BUT ROCKIE COULD CHANGE THAT! CARVE IT INTO FOUR PIECES.

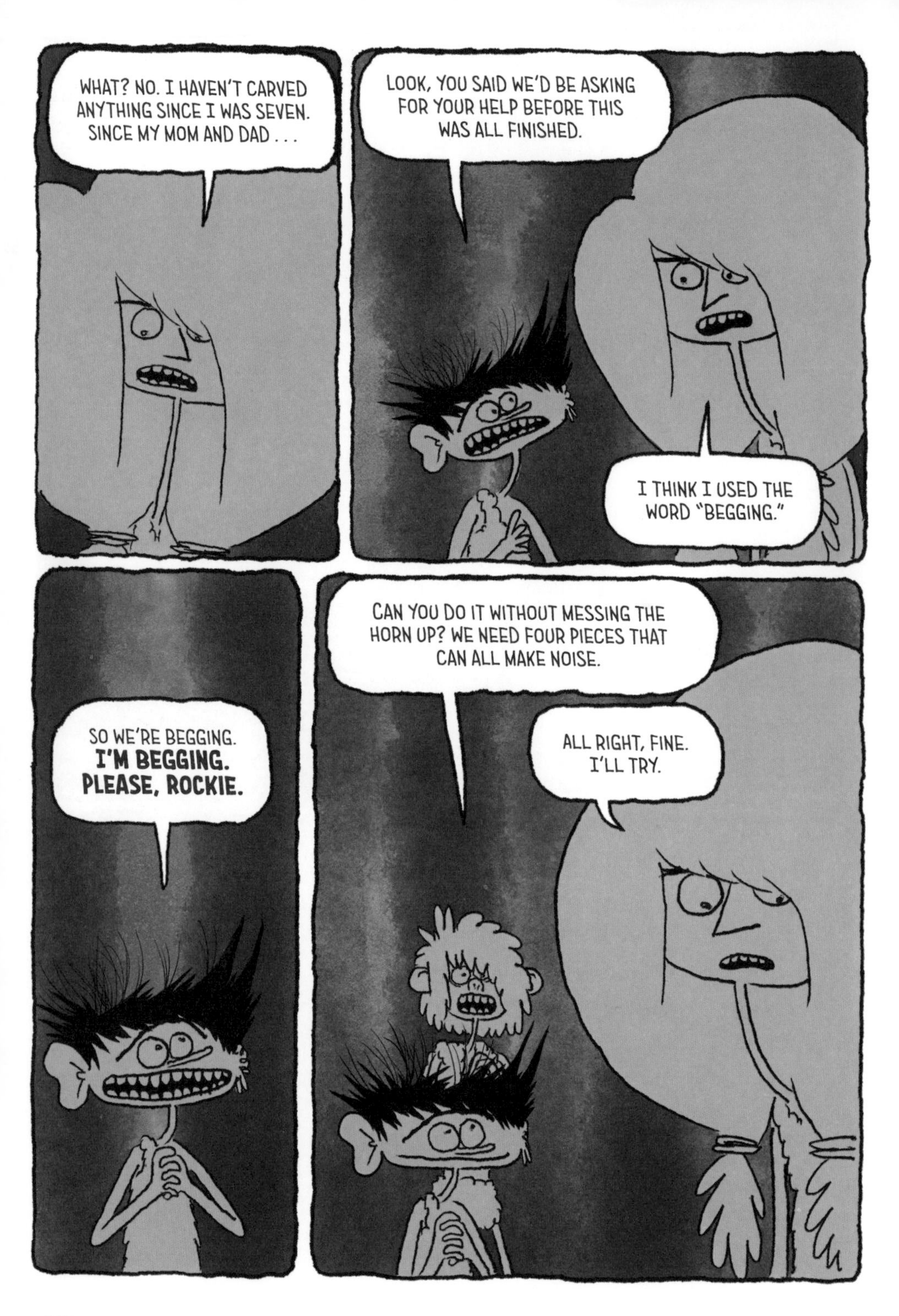
WHAT? NO. I HAVEN'T CARVED ANYTHING SINCE I WAS SEVEN. SINCE MY MOM AND DAD . . .
LOOK, YOU SAID WE'D BE ASKING FOR YOUR HELP BEFORE THIS WAS ALL FINISHED.
I THINK I USED THE WORD "BEGGING."
SO WE'RE BEGGING. **I'M BEGGING. PLEASE, ROCKIE.**
CAN YOU DO IT WITHOUT MESSING THE HORN UP? WE NEED FOUR PIECES THAT CAN ALL MAKE NOISE.
ALL RIGHT, FINE. I'LL TRY.

AND WE'RE GONNA NEED THAT ONE THING . . . WHAT'S IT CALLED? WHEN EVERYONE WORKS TOGETHER?
COOPERATION?
TEAMWORK?
SYNERGY?
THAT'S THE STUFF.
FOR THIS TO WORK, EVERYONE'S GOTTA DO THEIR THING. NO MORE MR. BOSSY BRITCHES.
WHAT BE BRITCHES?
WHAT BE PANTS?
I THINK THEY'RE LIKE PANTS.
NO IDEA.

Maybe Rockie was right. Maybe being the guy with all the ideas didn't have to be my thing.
ROCKIE'S THING IS TO FIX THE HORN.
ON IT!
I'd already lost my mom.
MR. UNGA-BUNGA, YOUR THING IS GETTING THE SHAMAN TO SAFETY.
ROGER THAT.
Maybe all that mattered was that I had my dad.
And my friends.
AND MY THING IS TO SAVE US ALL AND GET HOME TO MY LITTLE BABY FOO-FOO!

UG. I'M READY TO LISTEN.
TO WHAT?
YOUR PLAN.
OH, YEAH! MY PLAN!
YOU SURE, BRO? YOUR THING IS KINDA DANGEROUS.
DANGEROUS?
DAD.
I WAS JUST GOING TO SAY . . . THAT IT'S ABOUT TIME YOU GOT A LITTLE DANGEROUS.
ALL RIGHT, THEN. DANGEROUS, IT IS.
SWEET! 'CAUSE YOU GET TO BE **THE BAIT!**

DID YOU JUST SAY **"BAIT"?**
YOU GOT IT, AMIGO!
AWESOME. I'M ALL EARS. WELL . . . I'M ALL EAR.
THEN GATHER UP, COMPADRES! HERE'S WHAT I'M THINKING. . . .

Ug's plan was a good one. Using the horns to lure the rippy-beaks away from the village, like a relay race. . . .

We were a team, everybody playing their part.
Problem with a team, though. If somebody on the team dies before you reach the finish line . . . everyone loses.
Once everyone was clear on their positions, we set Ug's plan in motion.
HOW ARE YOU GONNA CLIMB ALL THE WAY TO THE TOP OF THIS, CLUNK?
EASY. CLUNK CLIMB. CLIMBING CLUNK'S THING.
Clunk had a talent for keeping it simple.
Clunk smash. Clunk eat. Clunk climb.

I needed to simplify.
Dave eat. Dave sleep. Dave never lead village again.
OKAY, CLUNK. YOU KNOW WHAT TO DO.
CLUNK KNOW. CLUNK HIDE.
IF ANY OF US SURVIVES THIS, I'LL SEE YOU AT THE END.
DAVE, BE CAREFUL.
EASY FOR YOU TO SAY. YOU'RE NOT THE BAIT.

THE FIRST HORN. THAT WAS DAD.
Either the plan was working perfectly or I was about to become an orphan with a seriously tragic backstory.
THAT'S ROCKIE.
HERE COMES BANE.
AND HERE COMES TROUBLE.
TRIANGLE!!!

RUN, UG.
AHHHHHHHHHH! I HATE BIRDS!!!
RUN, UG.
RUN, UG.
I GOT THIS.
DON'T LOOK BEHIND YOU!
WHY NOT?

I DON'T GOT THIS!!!
The rippy-beaks were focused on Ug.
WHY DID YOU LISTEN TO ME? THIS IS A TERRIBLE IDEA!
THEY DON'T SEE ME.

And without a horn of my own, I had no way to attract their attention.
LOOK UP HERE!
I TAKE IT BACK! DON'T LOOK UP HERE!!!
It was time to do my thing.
OKAY, BIG D.
So I jumped.

MAYBE THIS IS ACTUALLY GOING TO WORK.
THIS IS NEVER GOING TO WORK!

I had to stop looking and focus. This wasn't all about me. I had to do my part in this plan.
So I steered like crazy toward the one place I needed to be.
The one place I didn't want to go.

Straight into the Field of Screams.

12

RED! GREEN! ORANGE! BLACK! BLACK! BLUE! GREEN! ORANGE!

I just had to remember the order and steer.

The heat was carrying me too high. If this plan was going to work, I had to get down in the danger zone.
COME ON, FEATHER-DUSTER! COME AND GET ME!

BLUE . . .
GREEN . . .
ORANGE . . .
RED!

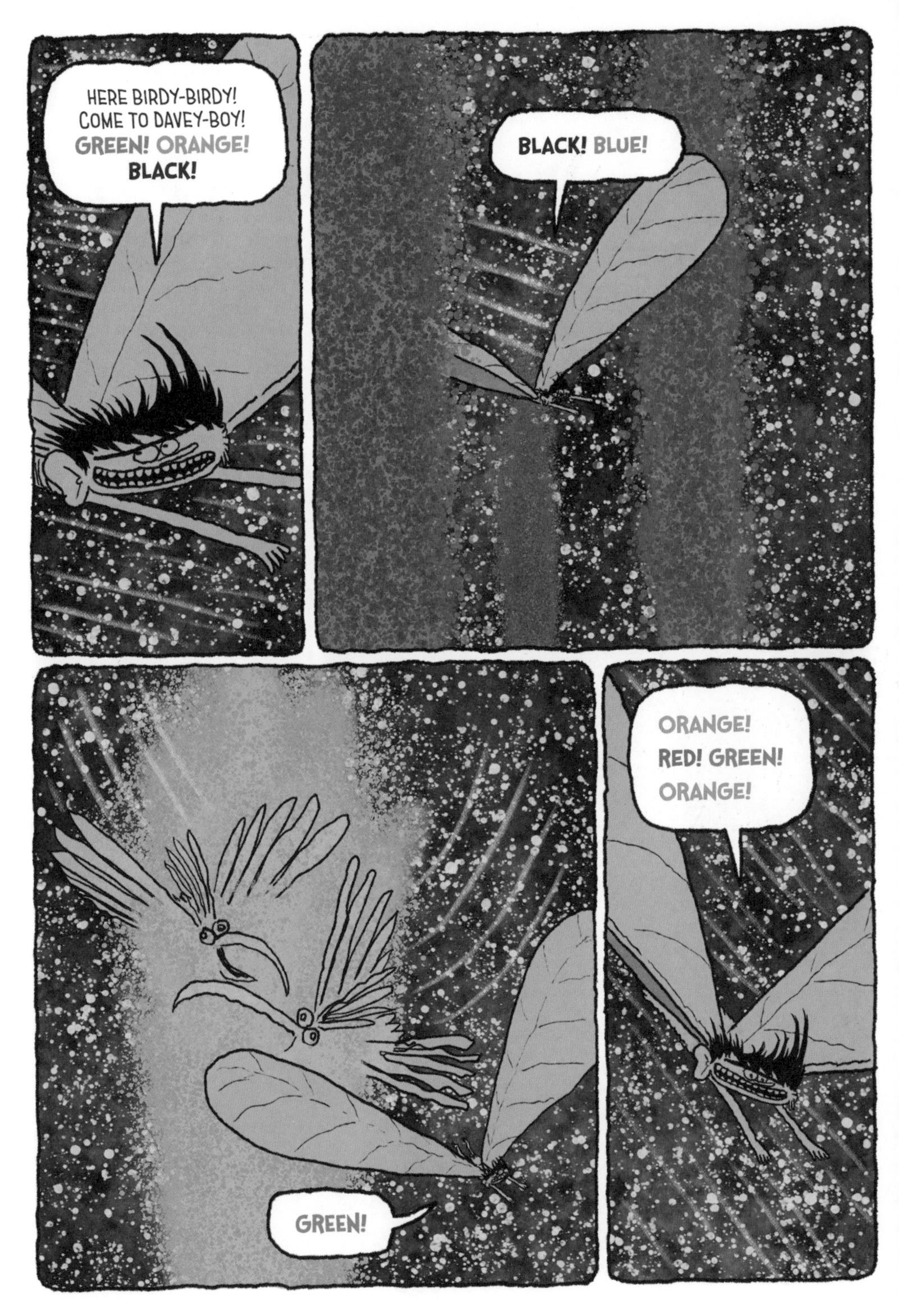
HERE BIRDY-BIRDY!
COME TO DAVEY-BOY!
GREEN! ORANGE!
BLACK!
BLACK! BLUE!
GREEN!
ORANGE!
RED! GREEN!
ORANGE!

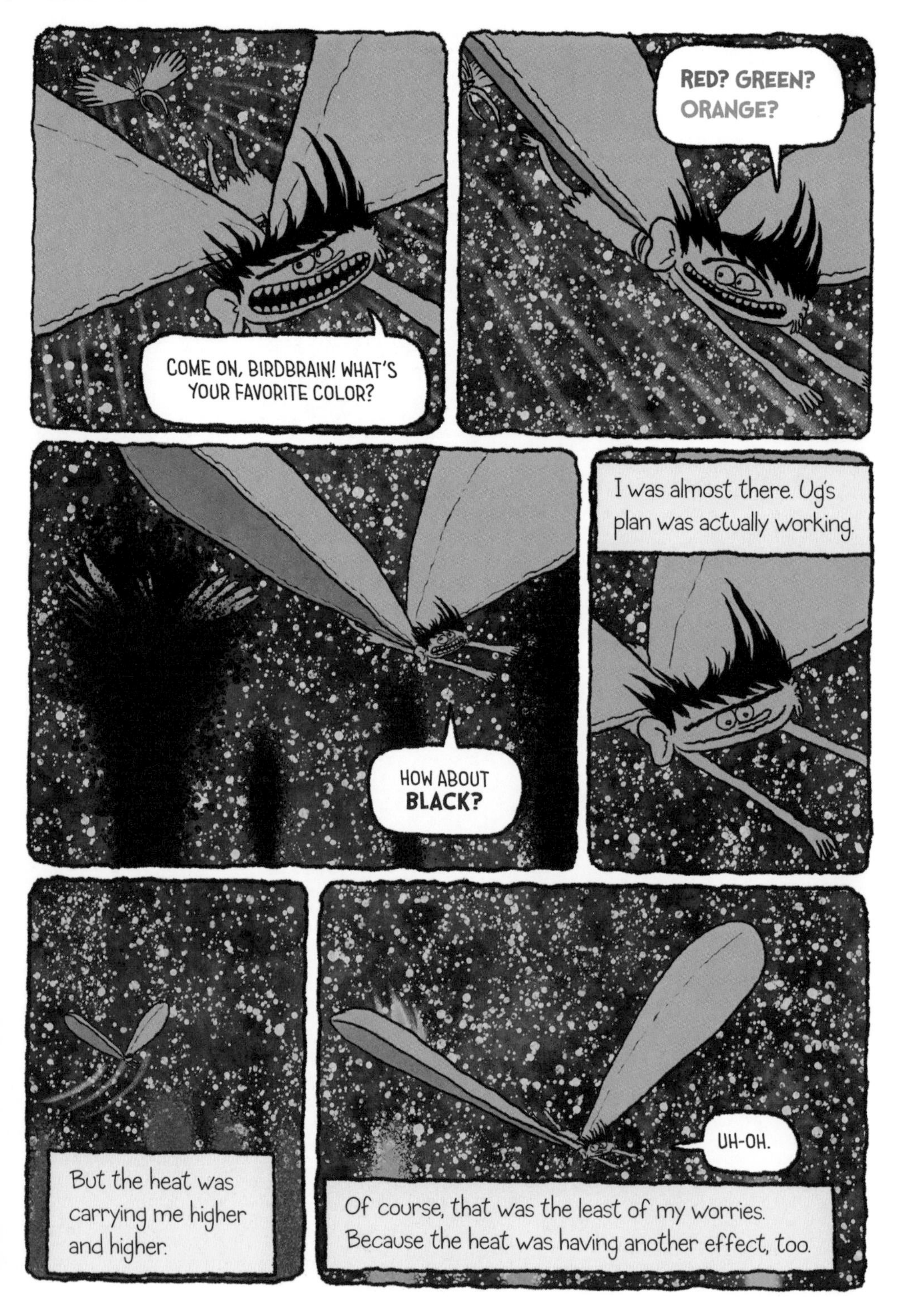
COME ON, BIRDBRAIN! WHAT'S YOUR FAVORITE COLOR?
RED? GREEN? ORANGE?
HOW ABOUT BLACK?
I was almost there. Ug's plan was actually working.
But the heat was carrying me higher and higher.
UH-OH.
Of course, that was the least of my worries. Because the heat was having another effect, too.

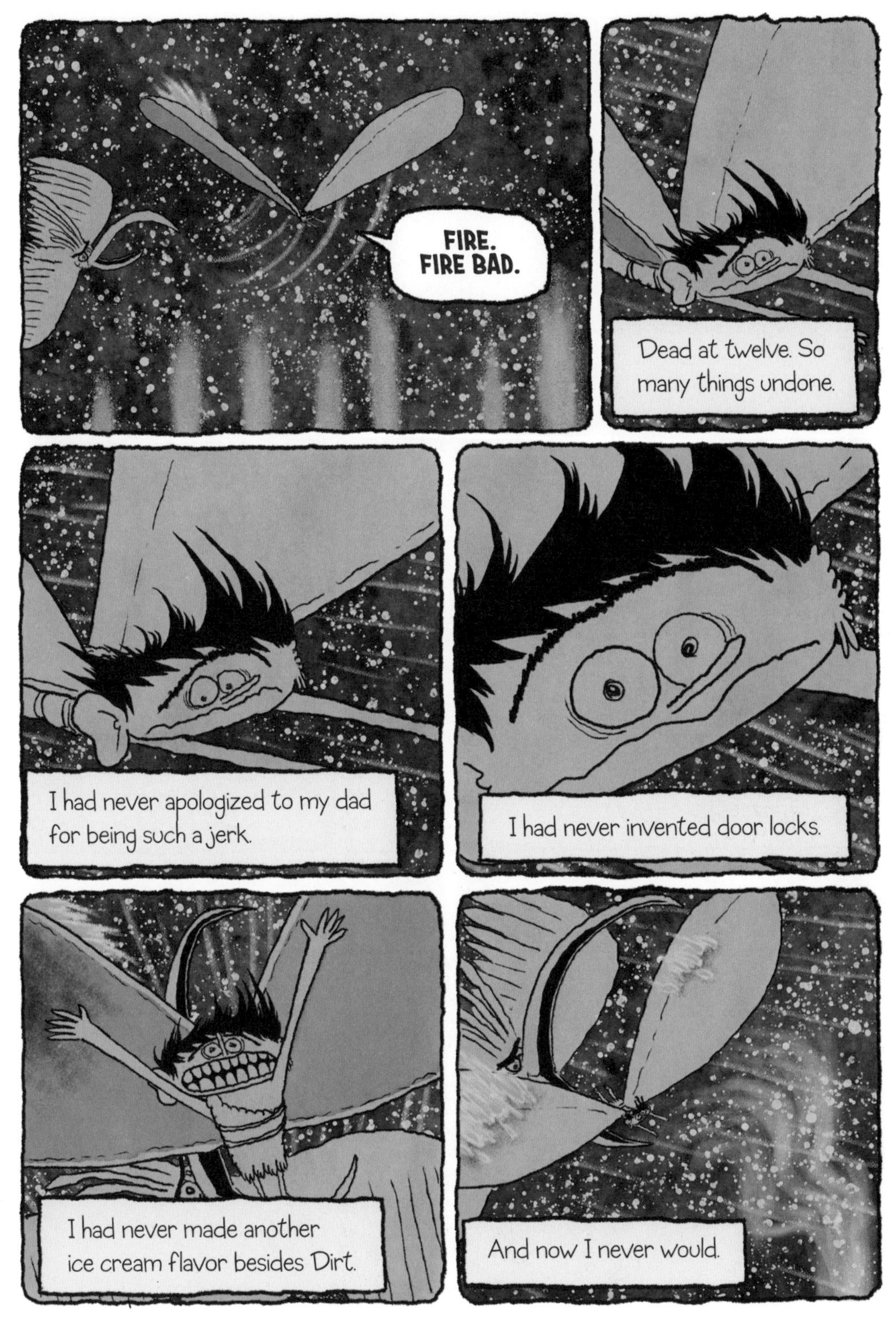
FIRE.
FIRE BAD.
Dead at twelve. So many things undone.
I had never apologized to my dad for being such a jerk.
I had never invented door locks.
I had never made another ice cream flavor besides Dirt.
And now I never would.

DAD!
Dad said I was trying so hard to do my own thing that I forgot to just be Dave.
And he was right.
If there's one thing Dave knew how to do, it was think on his feet.
EJECT
So that's what I did.

Of course, I'm not sure if "falling" can be considered thinking on your feet.
But it was all I had left.
Dad was still trying to protect me. But it was my turn to protect him for a change.
After all, Rockie was right. He was all I had.

I'M SORRY, DAD! FOR EVERYTHING!
WHAT ARE YOU DOING, BOY?
I was doing the one thing left to do.
The one thing that would make sure Dad and the others got away safely.
The one thing Rockie predicted I would do. Crash and burn.

A shaman didn't always need to have all the answers.
A good shaman listened.
And sometimes a shaman could just be there for his people.
Even unto death.
Hopefully I hadn't realized it too late.

YOU'RE! MESSING! UP!
MY! SUMMER! VACATION!

OKAY, YOU BIG CHICKEN.
END OF THE LINE.

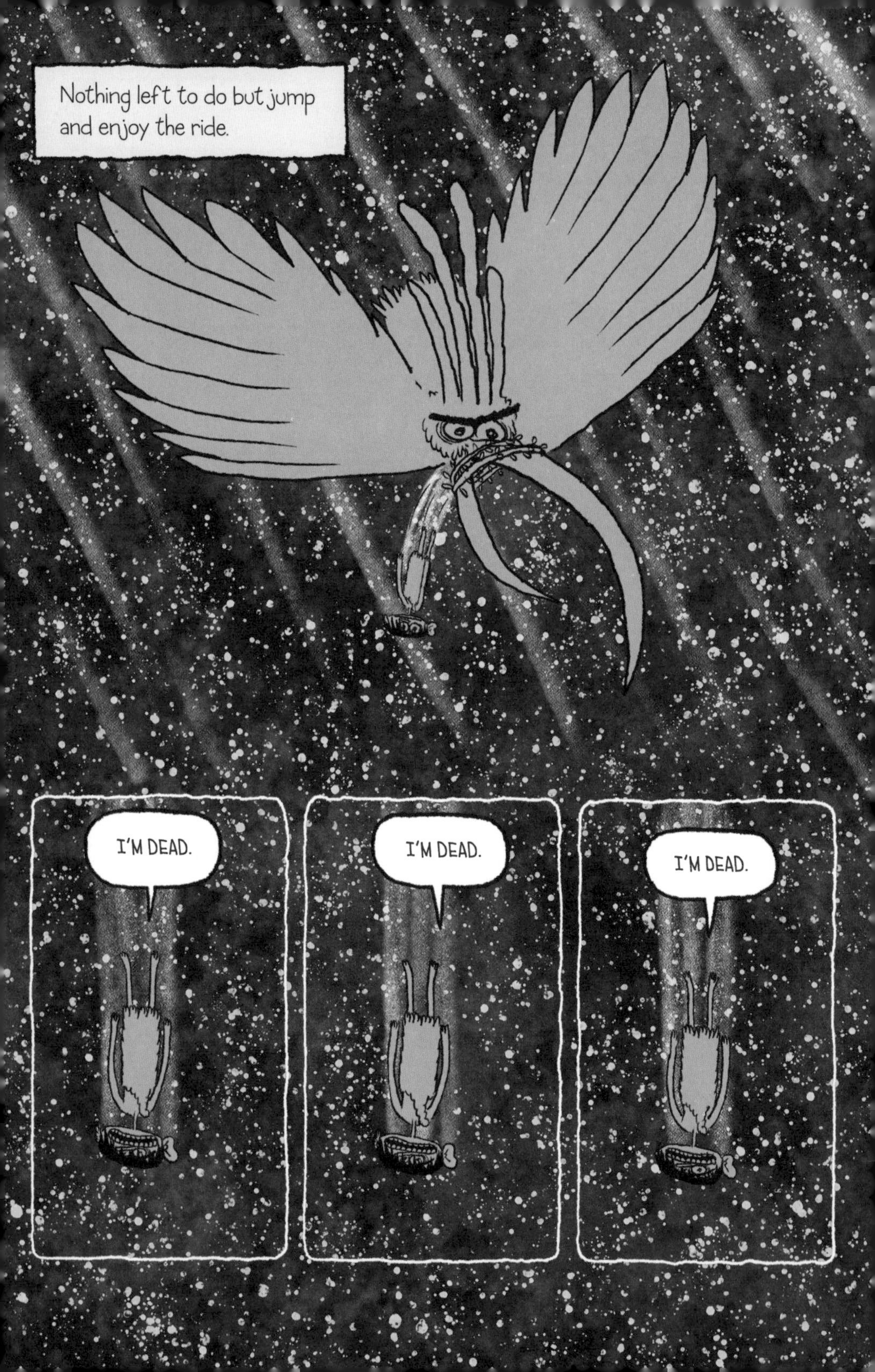
Nothing left to do but jump and enjoy the ride.
I'M DEAD.
I'M DEAD.
I'M DEAD.

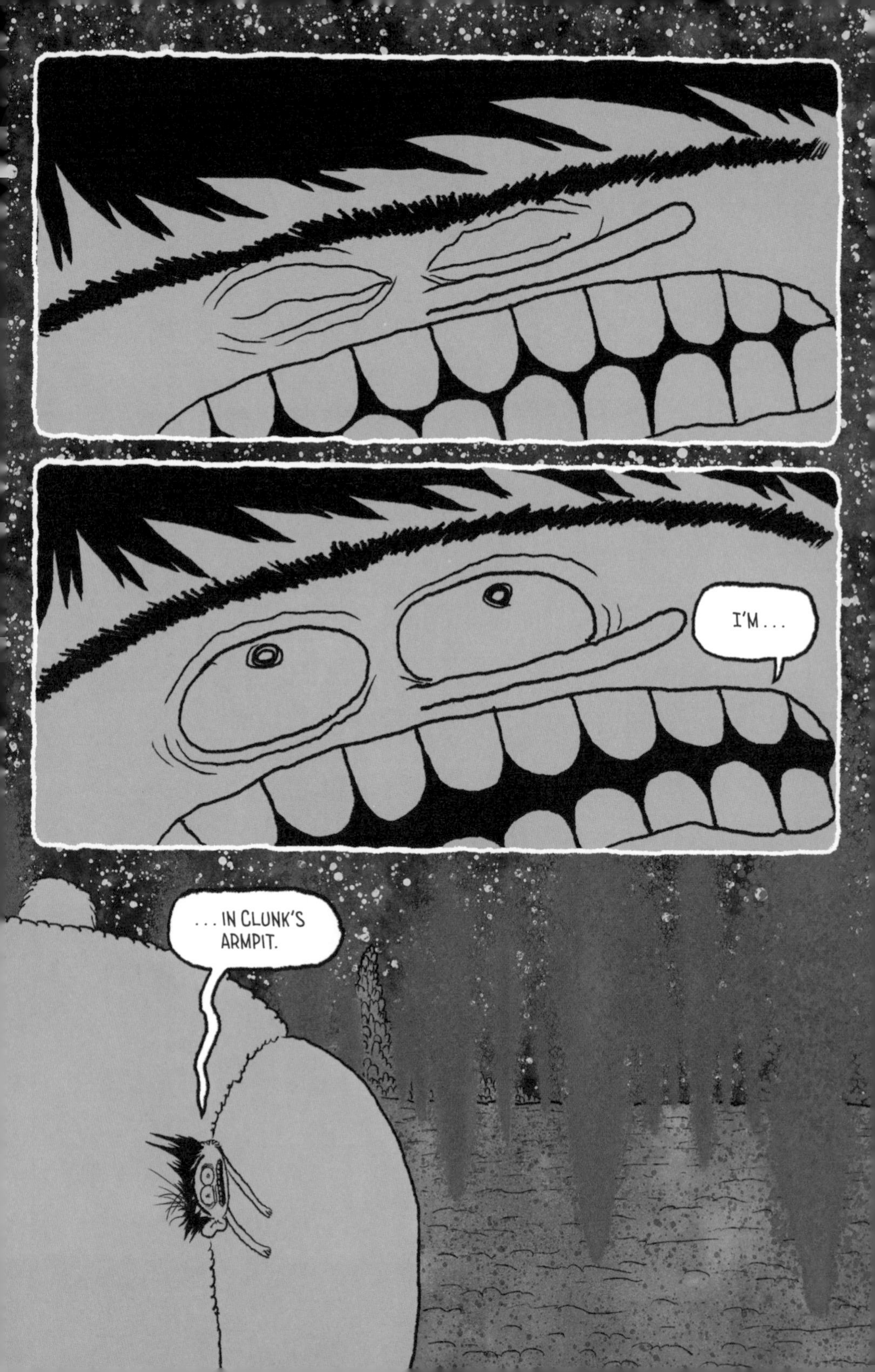
I'M . . .
. . . IN CLUNK'S ARMPIT.

YOU MADE IT, BRO! DON'T DO THAT TO ME AGAIN. MY TICKER CAN'T TAKE IT.
UNBELIEVABLE. MR. WONDERFUL ACTUALLY PULLED IT OFF.
BY THE UNIBROW OF DUM-DUM! YOU'RE ALIVE!
CLUNK CATCH DAVE.
YOU DID?
SNATCHED YOU RIGHT OUT OF THE AIR. YOU SHOULD'VE SEEN IT.

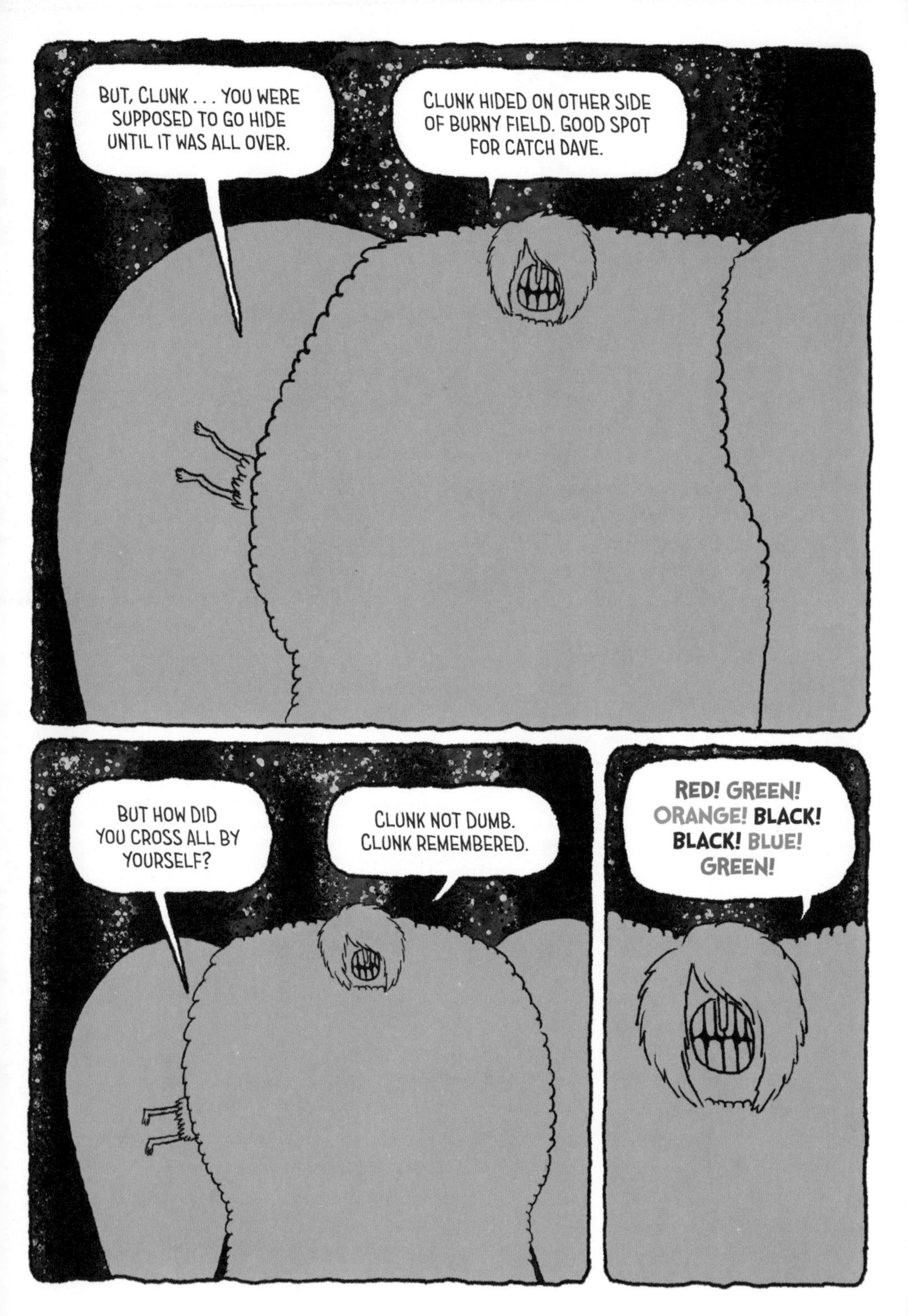
BUT, CLUNK . . . YOU WERE SUPPOSED TO GO HIDE UNTIL IT WAS ALL OVER.
CLUNK HIDED ON OTHER SIDE OF BURNY FIELD. GOOD SPOT FOR CATCH DAVE.
BUT HOW DID YOU CROSS ALL BY YOURSELF?
CLUNK NOT DUMB. CLUNK REMEMBERED.
RED! GREEN! ORANGE! BLACK! BLACK! BLUE! GREEN!

SKRAWWWK!
ONE MORE COLOR. WHAT IS?
SKRAWWWK?
OH, YEAH! ORANGE!

CAN YOU WALK, BOY?
I THINK SO.
DO YOU KNOW HOW DANGEROUS THAT WAS?!
YOU WERE AMAZING.
DAD, I'M SO SORRY.
ME TOO, LAD.

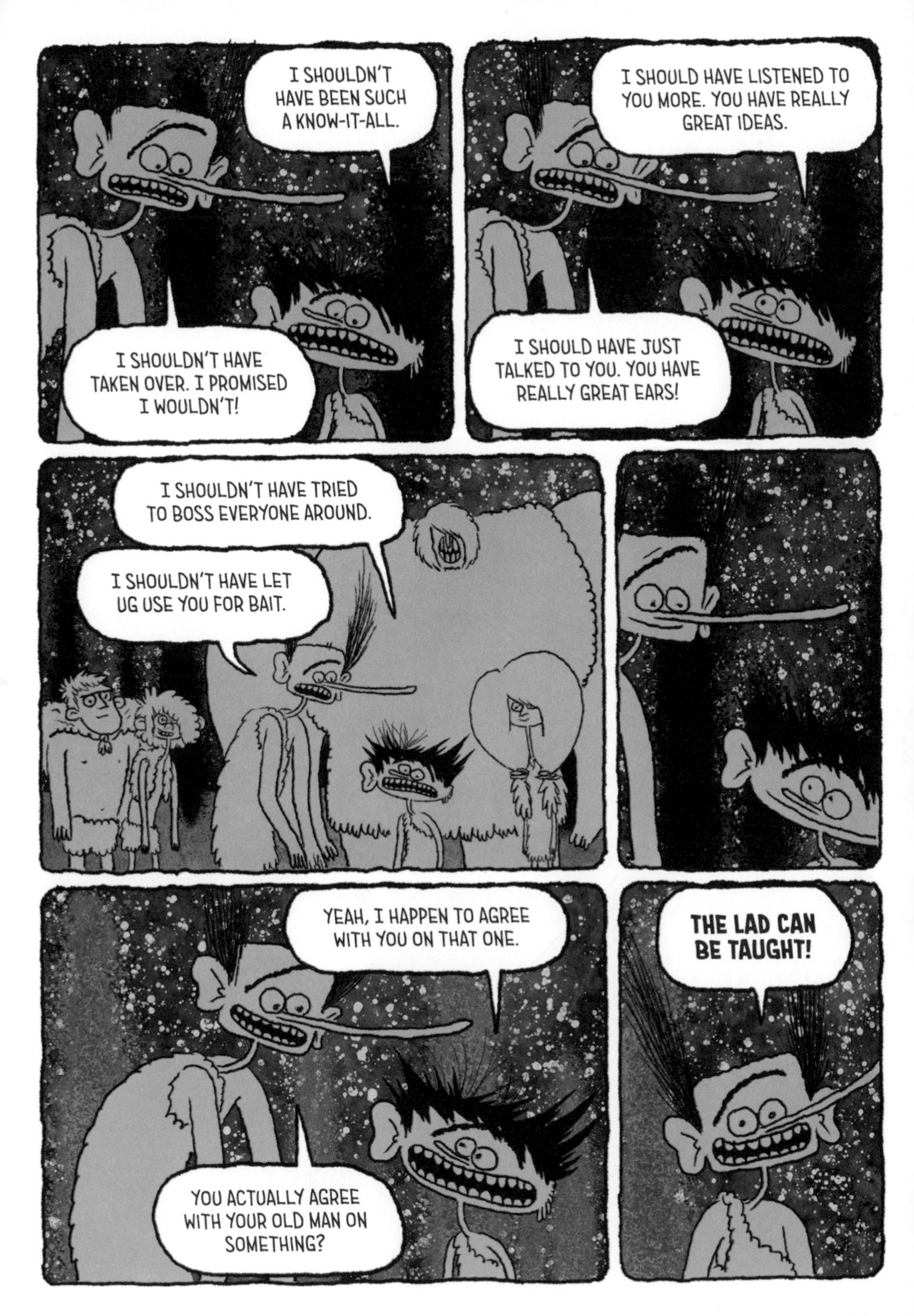
I SHOULDN'T HAVE BEEN SUCH A KNOW-IT-ALL.
I SHOULDN'T HAVE TAKEN OVER. I PROMISED I WOULDN'T!
I SHOULD HAVE LISTENED TO YOU MORE. YOU HAVE REALLY GREAT IDEAS.
I SHOULD HAVE JUST TALKED TO YOU. YOU HAVE REALLY GREAT EARS!
I SHOULDN'T HAVE TRIED TO BOSS EVERYONE AROUND.
I SHOULDN'T HAVE LET UG USE YOU FOR BAIT.
YEAH, I HAPPEN TO AGREE WITH YOU ON THAT ONE.
YOU ACTUALLY AGREE WITH YOUR OLD MAN ON SOMETHING?
THE LAD CAN BE TAUGHT!

HEY, LOOK! IT'S SHAMAN EMBER!
YOU HAVE SAVED US.
YOU WOULDN'T HAVE NEEDED SAVING IF IT HADN'T BEEN FOR ME.
THIS IS VERY TRUE.
BUT IF IT HADN'T BEEN FOR YOU, THE RIPPY-BEAKS MIGHT HAVE PLAGUED US FOR YEARS.
NOW WE ARE FREE OF THEM. MY PEOPLE ARE GRATEFUL TO YOU.
THANKS, SHAMAN EMBER.
I HOPE YOU FIND SHAMAN FABOO.

OH, MAN! WE STILL HAVEN'T FOUND SHAMAN FABOO.
AND IF YOU DO . . . GIVE HIM A KISS FROM ME.
NOT IT.
NOT IT.
NOT IT.
DAVE IN CHARGE. DAVE GIVE KISS.
As we prepared to head home, I was torn.
On one hand, I desperately hoped we found Shaman Faboo.
But if we did, I owed it to Shaman Ember to pass along that kiss.

So on the other hand, I hoped
we didn't find him. Ever.

13

SHAMAN
FABOO
GONE

Mr. Gronk was waiting for us when we arrived at the village the next day.

We were tired, hungry, and defeated.
WELL? I SEE YOU'RE STILL ALIVE.
FOO-FOO! MOMMY'S NEVER LEAVING HOME AGAIN! **I SWEAR!**
AND SHAMAN FABOO?
NO LUCK, HERSHEL.

COULDN'T GET ACROSS THE FIELD OF SCREAMS, EH?
NO, WE DID.
WHAT?
DAVE GOT US ACROSS. WE GOT ALL THE WAY TO THE VILLAGE.
THEY DON'T HAVE HIM.
SHAMAN FABOO SEEMS TO HAVE DISAPPEARED INTO THIN AIR.
NOW WHAT, BRAIN MAN?
I'M ALL OUT OF ANSWERS.
MAYBE HE DIED IN THE FIELD OF SCREAMS.
MAYBE.
GONE

ALL I KNOW IS "SHAMAN FABOO GONE." MAYBE FOR GOOD.
SHAMAN FABOO
GONE
YOU KNOW WHAT THAT MEANS, DON'T YOU, BOY?
NO.
SHAMAN FABOO
GONE
IT MEANS YOU MAY NEED TO TAKE CHARGE FOR GOOD.
So much for simplifying my life.
I was doomed.

DON'T LOOK SO GLUM, BOY. I'LL BE RIGHT BY YOUR SIDE.
SHAMAN FABOO
GONE
DO YOU REALLY THINK I CAN REPLACE SHAMAN FABOO?
NO. BUT YOU CAN BE DAVE.
I'D FOLLOW YOU, BRO. YOU'RE THE SMARTEST DUDE I KNOW.
I ADMIT IT . . . YOU'VE GOT BIG BRAINS.

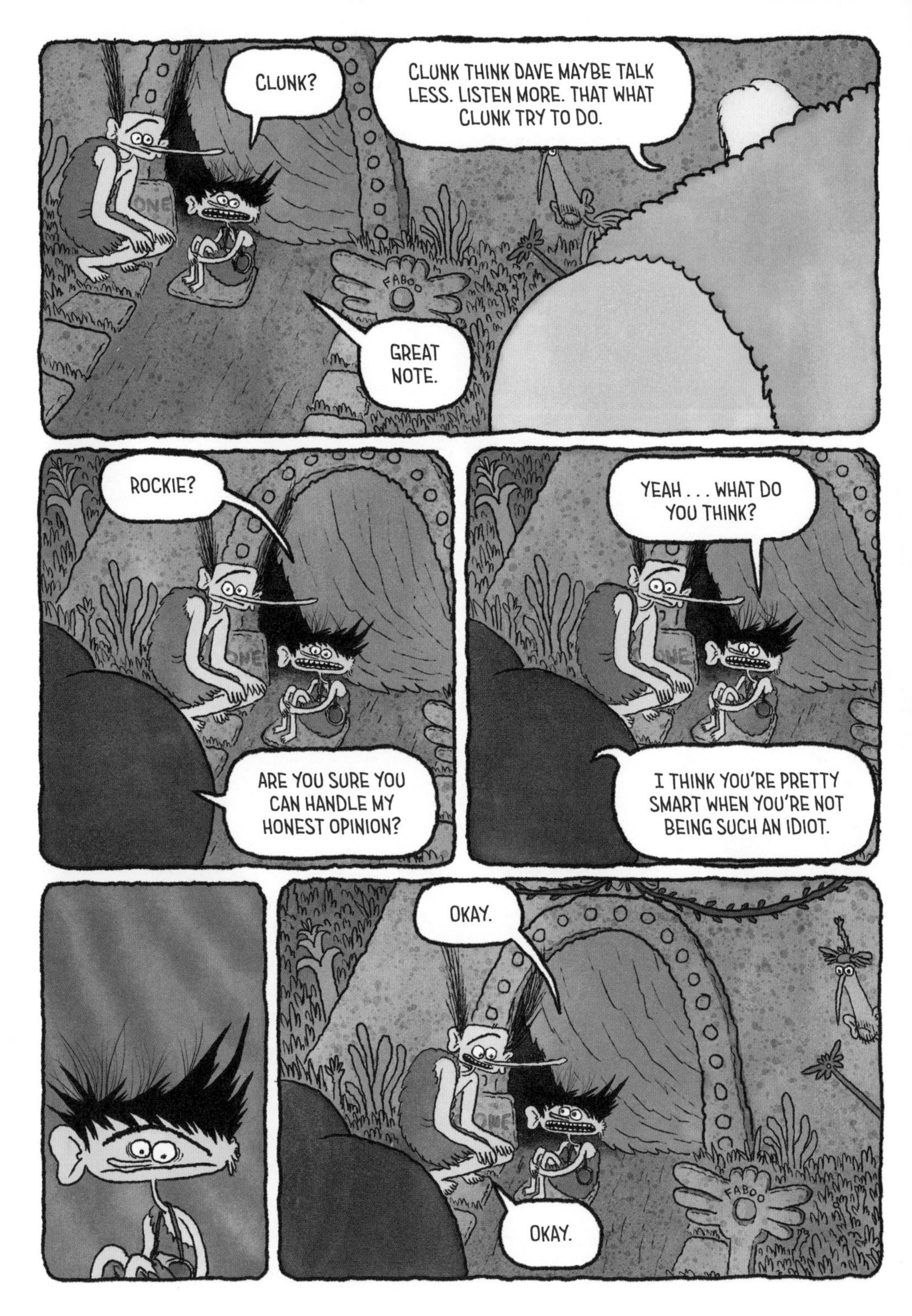
CLUNK?
CLUNK THINK DAVE MAYBE TALK LESS. LISTEN MORE. THAT WHAT CLUNK TRY TO DO.
FABOO
GREAT NOTE.
ROCKIE?
ARE YOU SURE YOU CAN HANDLE MY HONEST OPINION?
YEAH . . . WHAT DO YOU THINK?
I THINK YOU'RE PRETTY SMART WHEN YOU'RE NOT BEING SUCH AN IDIOT.
OKAY.
FABOO
OKAY.

BUT THE FIRST THING I NEED TO DO IS TELL THE VILLAGE ABOUT SHAMAN FABOO.
WHAT ARE YOU GOING TO TELL THEM?
ONE
THAT I COULDN'T FIND HIM.
ONE
NO. THAT *WE* COULDN'T FIND HIM.
OH, THAT'S TERRIBLE.
I KNOW. IT BREAKS MY HEART INTO LITTLE, TEENY PIECES.
I NEED TO TELL THEM THAT HE'S GONE FOR GOOD
IT'S SO SAD!
ONE
YEAH. IT'S NOT GONNA BE PRETTY.
WE'LL TELL THEM THAT DAVE IS TAKING CHARGE.

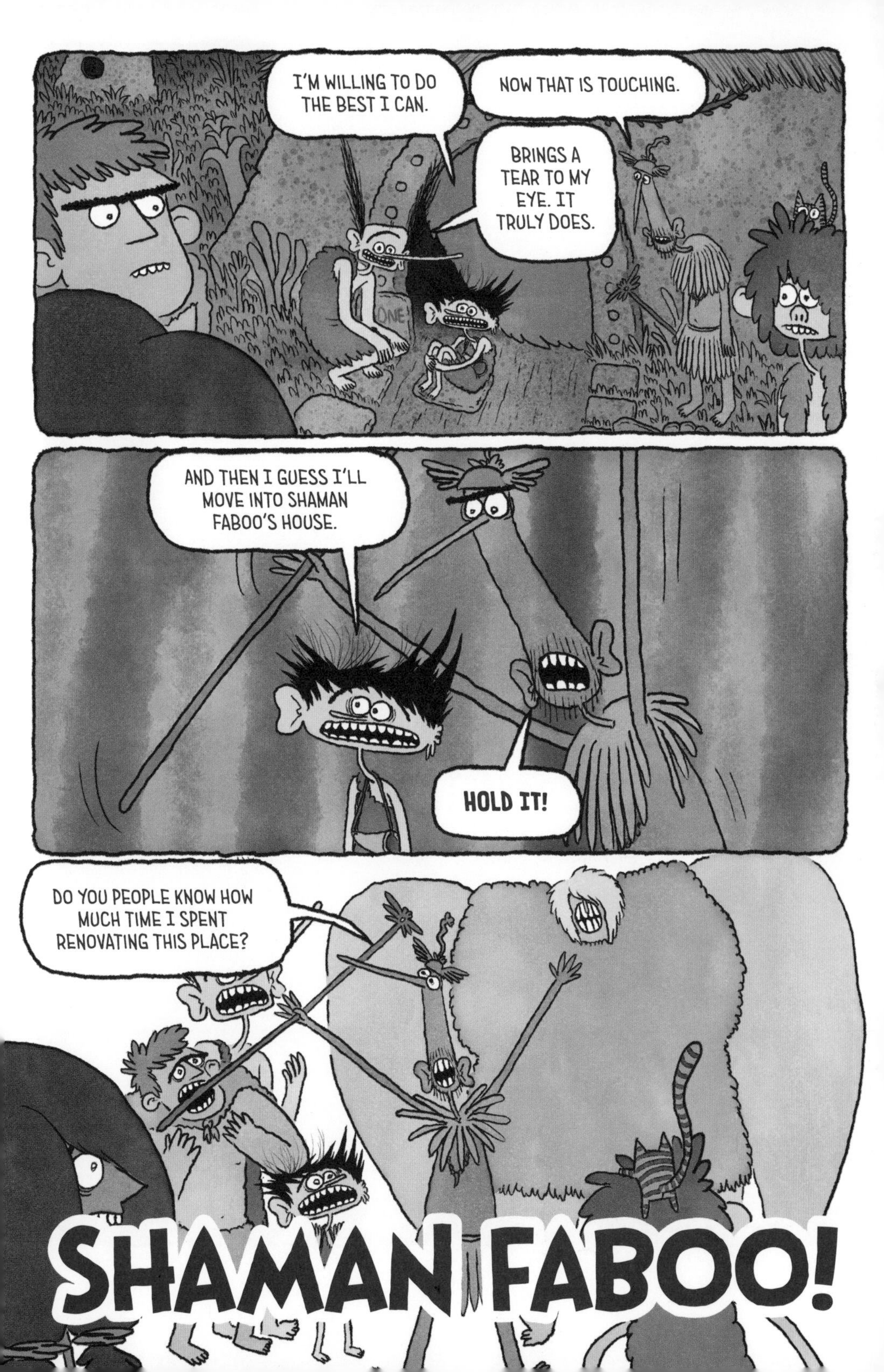
I'M WILLING TO DO THE BEST I CAN.
NOW THAT IS TOUCHING.
BRINGS A TEAR TO MY EYE. IT TRULY DOES.
ONE
AND THEN I GUESS I'LL MOVE INTO SHAMAN FABOO'S HOUSE.
HOLD IT!
DO YOU PEOPLE KNOW HOW MUCH TIME I SPENT RENOVATING THIS PLACE?
SHAMAN FABOO!

GAK RULES

I'M GONE A FEW DAYS AND YOU ARE PLANNING MY FUNERAL AND GIVING AWAY MY STUFF?
THAT STINGS, FOLKS.
HOORAY! SHAMAN FABOO IS BACK!
WELL, IT'S STINGING LESS NOW.
DIDN'T YOU GET MY NOTE?
YOUR NOTE?
WHY DID I SPEND ALL THAT TIME CHISELING IT IF NOBODY WAS GOING TO READ IT?
WE DID READ IT.
THEN YOU KNOW WHERE I'VE BEEN.

GONE? SHAMAN FABOO GONE?
IT'S A LITTLE VAGUE. EVEN FOR ME.
"SHAMAN FABOO"
SHAMAN FABOO
GONE
"GONE"
SHAMAN FABOO
GONE
"FISHING."
AH.
FISHING
CLUNK KNOW WHERE SHAMAN GONE.

I DIDN'T SEE THE OTHER PART OF THE NOTE. I THOUGHT YOU HAD BEEN KIDNAPPED.
FISHING
OBVIOUSLY NOT.
BUT CLUNK AND I TRACKED YOU! THERE WERE FOOTPRINTS.
YES. MINE!
AND SOMEBODY BEING DRAGGED.
SOMEBODY? YOU MEAN SOME*THING*.
YOU CAN'T GO FISHING WITHOUT YOUR BEST FISHING ROCKS, CAN YOU?
WHAT ARE YOU GOING TO HIT THE FISH WITH?
BUT TRACKS STOP.

YEAH. YOUR TRAIL DIDN'T LEAD TO FISHY POND. IT LED TO THE EDGE OF THE FIELD OF SCREAMS.
AH, THAT. LET'S JUST SAY I TOOK THE SCENIC ROUTE PAST THE GEYSERS.
I WAS SIMPLY HOPING TO CATCH A GLIMPSE OF SOMEONE . . . ER, SOMETHING ON THE OTHER SIDE.
DID YOU?
DID I WHAT?
CATCH A GLIMPSE OF HER. . . . I MEAN, IT?
NO.

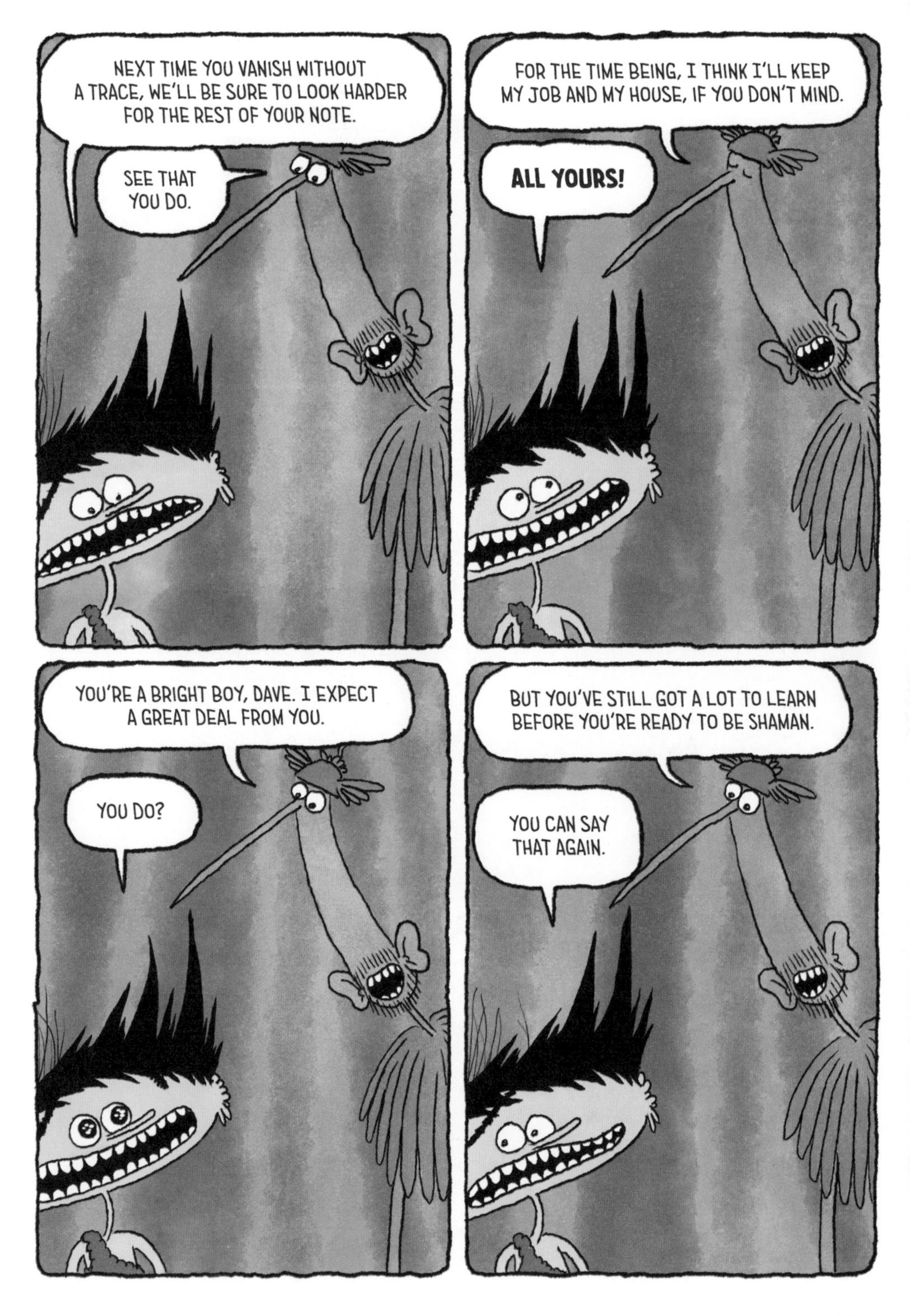
NEXT TIME YOU VANISH WITHOUT A TRACE, WE'LL BE SURE TO LOOK HARDER FOR THE REST OF YOUR NOTE.
SEE THAT YOU DO.
FOR THE TIME BEING, I THINK I'LL KEEP MY JOB AND MY HOUSE, IF YOU DON'T MIND.
ALL YOURS!
YOU'RE A BRIGHT BOY, DAVE. I EXPECT A GREAT DEAL FROM YOU.
YOU DO?
BUT YOU'VE STILL GOT A LOT TO LEARN BEFORE YOU'RE READY TO BE SHAMAN.
YOU CAN SAY THAT AGAIN.

I'LL TAKE THOSE FISH, SHAMAN. WE'LL GET A NICE BONFIRE GOING TO CELEBRATE YOUR RETURN.
OH, THAT WOULD BE LOVELY.
AND . . . I BAGGED A BABY SLUGASAURUS ON THE WAY HOME.
SHAMAN HUNT SLUGASAURUS ALL BY HIMSELF?
WHAT CAN I SAY, CLUNK? I'M A SHAMAN OF MANY SKILLS.
WAIT! YOU'RE NOT SHAMAN YET! I HAVE ONE MORE RESPONSIBILITY BEFORE I HAND THINGS BACK OVER TO YOU.
AND WHAT'S THAT?

SMOOCH
DID I JUST SEE WHAT I JUST SAW?
YOU SAW, BRO. YOU SAW.
DAVE, I'M TOUCHED THAT YOU MISSED ME.
IT'S NOT FROM ME!!!
IT'S FROM SHAMAN EMBER.
YOU . . . I . . . SHE . . .

HOW DO YOU KNOW ABOUT SHAMAN EMBER?!
IT'S A LONG STORY, SHAMAN.
I'LL MAKE US A CUP OF SLUDGEWATER TEA AND TELL YOU ALL ABOUT IT.
COME ON, EVERYBODY. LET'S GET THAT BONFIRE STARTED.
WE CELEBRATE WITH FISH TONIGHT!
CLUNK NOT LIKE FISH. TASTES LIKE FISH.
YOU'LL EAT IT AND YOU'LL LIKE IT.
CLUNK EAT. CLUNK NOT LIKE.

HEY! THIS SLUGASAURUS GOO IS SUPER-YUMMY!
DO YOU ALWAYS HAVE TO PUT EVERYTHING IN YOUR MOUTH?
IF I DIDN'T, I WOULDN'T KNOW HOW YUMMY THIS GOO IS, DORK!
HERE! TRY SOME!
THAT'S SOME PRETTY YUMMY GOO.
I'M BACK WITH FOO-FOO. YOU TWO ARE ARGUING. EVERYTHING'S BACK TO NORMAL.
NOT QUITE BACK TO NORMAL.
GIVE ME SOME OF THAT GOO.
TOLD YOU IT WAS AMAZING GOO!
I'LL SEE YOU GUYS LATER.

SO SHAMAN FABOO WAS JUST FISHING THE WHOLE TIME. FUNNY, HUH?
YEAH, FUNNY. YOU PUT EVERYONE IN DANGER FOR NOTHING.
YOU'RE RIGHT. BUT THAT'S NOT EVEN THE WORST PART.
WHAT WAS THE WORST PART?
I ONLY **ALMOST** HURT THEM.
BUT I **REALLY** HURT YOU.

DO YOU HAVE ANY IDEA WHAT A JERK YOU WERE TO ME?
YEAH.
I'M SORRY.
WHAT WAS THAT?
I'M SORRY.

HOLD ON.
HERE.
WHAT'S THIS?
SOMETHING I RECENTLY INVENTED. FOR YOU.
YOU INVENTED SOMETHING FOR ME?
YEAH. BUT IT WAS YOUR IDEA.

THAT'S REALLY GOOD. GOOEY.
AS SOON AS I TASTED THAT SLUGASAURUS GOO, I THOUGHT OF YOU.
HOW TOUCHING.
IT'S SOMETHING NEW. CALLED "MARSHMALLOWS."
MARSHMALLOW AND DIRT ICE CREAM. WHAT ARE YOU GOING TO CALL THIS NEW FLAVOR?
I THINK I'M GOING TO CALL IT . . .
ROCKIE ROAD.
GOOD NAME.
YEAH.

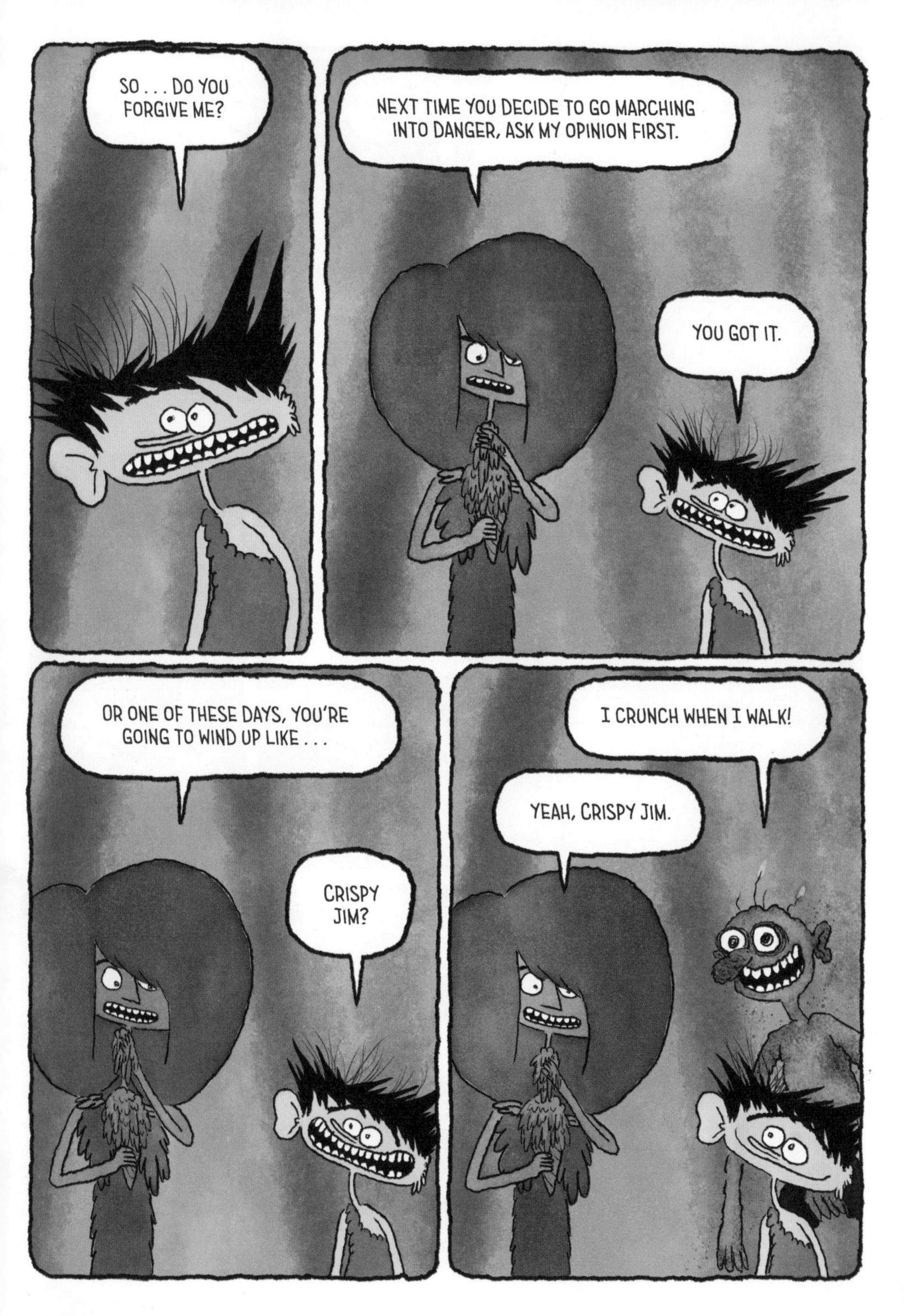
SO . . . DO YOU FORGIVE ME?
NEXT TIME YOU DECIDE TO GO MARCHING INTO DANGER, ASK MY OPINION FIRST.
YOU GOT IT.
OR ONE OF THESE DAYS, YOU'RE GOING TO WIND UP LIKE . . .
CRISPY JIM?
I CRUNCH WHEN I WALK!
YEAH, CRISPY JIM.

HEY, BIG D. THIS ICE CREAM NEEDS SOMETHING.
LIKE WHAT?
YOU REMEMBER THOSE PODS WE FOUND ON THAT TREE A COUPLE WEEKS AGO?
WITH THE YUMMY BROWN SEEDS INSIDE?
YEAH. WHAT'S THE NAME YOU GAVE THAT STUFF?
CHOCOLATE.
YEAH. NEEDS CHOCOLATE.
YOU WANT TO CHANGE MY NEW FLAVOR?

WHAT DO YOU THINK, BIG D?
I THINK IT'S A GREAT IDEA.
Leave it to Rockie to keep me on my toes.

And thank goodness for that.
PHIL '18

STARRING . . .
DAVE UNGA-BUNGA (Me!)
MR. UNGA-BUNGA
(My dad.)
BLA UNGA-BUNGA
(My sister.)
ROCKIE FIREGOOD
(She keeps me on my toes.)
UG SMITH
(He's 100% Ug. . . .)

BANE BONESNAP
(75% chest hair,
23% muscle, 2% brain.)

CLUNK
(Clunk smash. Clunk climb.
Clunk save my butt!)

SHAMAN FABOO
(Leader of Bleccchh . . .
unless he's gone fishing.)

OUR VILLAGE
(They like to panic.)

SHAMAN EMBER
(Leader and fearless defender
against rippy-beaks.)

SHAMAN EMBER'S VILLAGE
(Not scary bird-people.
They're just people like us!)